"I'm Anna Rose Palmer," She Said. "Introduce Yourself And We Won't Be Strangers."

"Britt Cameron." He watched her closely for a reaction. After all, it was possible that she'd heard about the murder trial.

"Pleased to meet you, Britt Cameron."

Britt was glad she hadn't recognized his name, relieved that he wouldn't be sent back out into the dark, rainy night . . . alone. He turned and left the room, wondering if he should tell her who he was. *She has a right to know that I was an accused murderer and that half of my hometown still thinks I killed my wife.*

As he walked away, Anna couldn't stop wondering about Britt—the man who'd wrecked his truck in front of her house. Odd—wasn't it?—that she'd just been thinking about needing a temporary man in her life, someone she could pass off as her mystery fiancé, and then, *poof,* out of nowhere, this tall, dark stranger had appeared . . . .

Dear Reader:

Welcome to Silhouette Desire! If this is your first Desire novel, I hope it will be the first of many, but if you are a regular reader, you'll already know that you're in for a treat.

This month we have a special selection of six, sexy men to warm up your winter! You'll find them fascinating, stubborn, independent and *desirable*—we guarantee it!

Every Desire this month has the portrait of a gorgeous guy on the cover, and we're confident you'll enjoy seeing all of these handsome heroes receive their just deserts.

Go on, indulge yourself—you deserve it!

Jane Nicholls
Silhouette Books
PO Box 236
Thornton Road
Croydon
Surrey
CR9 3RU

BEVERLY BARTON
CAMERON

Silhouette Desire

Originally Published by Silhouette Books
a division of
Harlequin Enterprises Ltd.

*First published in Great Britain in 1993
by Silhouette Books, Eton House, 18-24 Paradise Road,
Richmond, Surrey TW9 1SR*

© Beverly Beaver 1993

*Silhouette, Silhouette Desire and Colophon are
Trade Marks of Harlequin Enterprises B.V.*

ISBN 0 373 59055 5

22-9312

Made and printed in Great Britain

BEVERLY BARTON

has been in love with romance since her grandfather gave her an illustrated book of *Beauty and the Beast*. An avid reader since childhood, she began writing at the age of nine, and wrote short stories, poetry, plays and novels throughout school and college. After marriage to her own "hero" and the births of her daughter and son, she chose to be a full-time homemaker, a.k.a. wife, mother, friend and volunteer.

Six years ago, she began substitute teaching and returned to writing as a hobby. Her hobby became an obsession as she devoted more and more time to improving her skills as a writer. Now, her lifelong dream of being published has come true.

Other Silhouette Books by Beverly Barton

Silhouette Desire

Yankee Lover
Lucky in Love
Out of Danger
Sugar Hill
Talk of the Town
The Wanderer

Prologue

With one hand Britt Cameron gripped the steering wheel of his truck and with the other he tilted the half-empty cola can up to his mouth.

At first he hadn't even noticed that it was raining, but when his visibility through the windshield of the mud-splattered old Chevy became completely obscured, he'd turned on the windshield wipers. The scraping beat of the wipers swishing away the heavy raindrops blended with Clint Black's country drawl belting out his latest hit tune. The radio's high volume didn't bother Britt, nor did the loud booms of thunder blasting overhead. The more noise, the better. Perhaps it would block out the memories—the pain—the *fear*.

He took another deep swig from the can, then tossed the empty container onto the floorboard. Wiping his mouth with the back of his hand, he felt the heavy scars that covered his flesh. Quickly he glanced down at his hands. Both were covered with puckered skin and the fingers on his left hand were gnarled, the two middle fingers braided together like a knot.

He ran his deformed hand up the side of his face, the left side. From his left cheekbone to his neck, strips of torn flesh had healed into scars. Scars that he had refused to let a plastic surgeon touch.

For three years after the accident that had killed his best friend and changed his own life forever, Britt had thought that nothing worse could ever happen to him.

He'd been wrong.

For endless weeks he had sat in that courtroom and felt the curious stares of the jurors, and had wondered if they would believe him capable of murder. Tortured weeks when he hadn't known if they would convict him or set him free. Finally he'd reached the point where the verdict no longer mattered. His life became meaningless. He had already lost everything but his freedom.

The past eighteen months of his life had been a nightmare from which he didn't think he would ever awaken. From the day his wife had run off with Reverend Charles, fate had set Britt on a path of destruction.

Now that the trial was over, he didn't know where he was going or what he was going to do. He didn't care anymore. Nothing mattered.

The 10:00 p.m. news report came on the radio. Britt longed for a drink, something much stronger than the sugary, caffeinated cola he'd just consumed. But he never drank when he drove, not even before the accident, and certainly not afterward.

"Today in Riverton, Mississippi, accused murderer Britt Cameron was acquitted of all charges in the tragic death of his estranged wife. Tanya Cameron, who had left her husband six months prior to her death, was found dead in his trailer over a year ago. Ms. Cameron died from a severe head wound. The prosecution claimed that, in a fit of jealous rage, Cameron had followed through on his threat to kill—"

Britt flipped off the radio. The rain was getting progressively heavier. He considered pulling off to the side of the road, but didn't want to stop. He had to keep going, keep moving. He had to get away from Riverton, and all those accusing stares, all the whispered innuendos.

He crossed the Mississippi line over into Alabama, his foot light on the gas pedal as he slowed the truck's speed down to a crawl. Paying little attention to where he was driving, and not caring a hoot about his destination, Britt turned off the main highway onto a side road. As the rain fell in never ending rivulets, the road ahead curved into the hills outside of Cherokee. Houses became few and far between. Cultivated farmland, dense woods and a black sky rioting with a thunderstorm surrounded Britt.

Suddenly a deer dashed across the road in front of him. His only thought to avoid colliding with the animal, Britt slammed on his brakes. The truck swerved, hitting a dangerously slick spot on the pavement, then slid across the road and into a deep ditch. The last coherent thought Britt had before his head hit the windshield was that, as long as he lived, he'd never love and trust another woman.

One

A crackle of earsplitting thunder shook the old farmhouse moments before a blaze of brilliant lightning zigzagged through the night sky. Nestling more snugly into the softness of the plump, chintz-covered sofa, Anna Rose pressed her open book against her breasts. Lying at her feet on a hand-braided rug, Lord Byron growled as if the threatening rumble from his massive chest would frighten away the storm. Anna Rose dropped her hand to the rottweiler's head, patting him tenderly as she whispered baby-talk words of comfort.

Bringing the book away from her body, Anna Rose adjusted herself and her treasured volume of verse and prose so that she could see better in the dim light from the kerosene lamp. Thunderstorms had ravaged the state this spring, and even now, in late May, seemed determined to add more destruction to the flood conditions in Alabama. Thankfully tomorrow was Saturday, so, even though the road into

Cherokee was blocked from the night's deluge, she wouldn't have to worry about making it in to school.

Centering her attention on the printed word, Anna Rose read the poem, silently at first and then aloud. Marlowe's "The Passionate Shepherd to his Love" was one of her favorites. How many years had she spent longing to hear a man speak such words to her? To ask her to come with him and be his love?

Flipping through the pages, she paused at a section entitled "Unrequited Love". She took a deep breath, releasing it slowly as she ran the tip of her tongue over the edges of her teeth. Willing herself not to cry again, she tightened her throat, trapping the tears. As Anna Rose began to read, it seemed that Lord Alfred Douglas's "Two Loves" was printed in large bold type, so poignant were the words.

Slamming the book closed, she tossed it to the other end of the sofa. "Tarnation! Double, triple tarnation!"

She had to stop this—and now. No more feeling sorry for herself. No more condemning herself for acting like an idiot. After all, she wasn't the first woman who'd made a fool of herself over a man.

"But did you have to lie to the whole town?" she asked herself aloud, shaking her head in disgust.

When Kyle had announced his engagement to his college sweetheart, Anna Rose had become the object of everyone's pity. And pity was one thing she couldn't abide. She'd received far too much of that misplaced emotion in her twenty-seven years. Poor Anna Rose, whose teenage, unwed mother had committed suicide at the age of seventeen. Poor Anna Rose, such a plain, plump wallflower. Poor Anna Rose, who'd had total responsibility for the care of her aging grandparents before their deaths. Poor Anna Rose would make such a good wife and mother, but no man wanted her. It wasn't just because she was no great beauty. Plainer women had married. No. Anna Rose knew that she intimidated most men. Not only was she fiercely independent and a trifle too bossy, but folks in Cherokee said she was too smart, far smarter than any of the men in town. And no man wanted a wife smarter than he was.

Anna Rose stood, stretched her arms above her head and looked down at Lord Byron, who was staring up at her. "I'm hungry. How about you?" Rounding the couch, she picked up the kerosene lamp from the long library table that flanked the back wall and started toward the hallway. "There's some fried chicken left. How about a drumstick all your own?"

The enormous dog came quickly to his feet, following his mistress out into the long, wide hallway that spanned the length of the house from front to back.

After entering the kitchen, Anna Rose placed the lamp in the center of the blue-gingham-covered table. "You know what I need, Lord Byron?" She watched as the big animal slumbered over toward the refrigerator and flopped down, waiting for her to open the door. "I need a man."

Lord Byron stared up at her, his brown eyes bright and alert. Anna Rose opened the refrigerator, retrieved a plate of cold chicken and placed it on the table before seating herself in the straight-back wooden chair. "I made a total fool of myself over Kyle when he first came to town last year. Of course, all the unmarried teachers did. Not just me."

She removed the aluminum foil from the plate, picked up a drumstick and took a bite. Lord Byron moaned. "Oh, all right. Here you go." When she handed him his own piece of chicken, the dog's enormous mouth opened to accept the late-night treat. "Don't you dare leave the kitchen with that," she warned.

Anna Rose munched on the cold chicken as she listened to the torrential downpour and the occasional roar of thunder that seemed to be moving farther and farther away. "I should have had better sense. After all, I'm so darn smart. I'm a school principal, aren't I? I'm practically going on thirty. I should have known that Kyle thought of me as nothing more than a good friend."

Lord Byron wasn't paying much attention to his mistress's ramblings. He was far too busy devouring his treat.

Anna Rose scooted her chair over to the cabinet, removed a dish towel from a drawer and wiped her hands and mouth. "What I need, Lord Byron, is a fiancé. A temporary fiancé."

Licking his lips, the rottweiler cocked his head to one side as if recognizing the word *fiancé*. Anna Rose laughed. "Yeah, I've been saying that word a lot lately, haven't I?"

If only she hadn't overreacted when Kyle had married and the whole town began whispering behind her back. If only she hadn't told her friend Edith Hendricks that people were silly to think she'd been seriously interested in Kyle Ross. After all, she, too, had a secret fiancé, a man she'd met on vacation the previous year who'd been writing and phoning her on a regular basis.

"Me and my big mouth," Anna Rose said. "That was nearly two months ago, and folks are wondering why my mysterious fiancé hasn't shown up."

Suddenly Lord Byron stood, his big body tense, his nose pointing in the air and his ears set back as he listened. Like a small, galloping horse, the rottweiler ran from the kitchen, his loud, leonine bark echoing in the long hallway.

"What in tarnation's the matter with you?" Anna Rose picked up the lamp and followed quickly, wondering just what had upset Lord Byron.

The dog stood at the front door, one big paw scratching—his signal for wanting outside. As Anna Rose neared, she set the lamp on the seat of a massive oak hall tree. "What's the matter, boy? Did you hear something?" She seriously doubted that she had late visitors, especially on a night like this.

Opening the front door, Anna Rose braced herself for the blast of damp air. The high wind whipped through the trees and blew rain across the wide front porch. Peering outside through the screen door, she saw nothing but the black night sky and heard only the wind and the rain.

"There's nothing there, boy. See?" The minute she eased the screen door open slightly, Lord Byron lunged, pushing past Anna Rose and out onto the porch. He emitted several loud howls, galloped out into the yard, then disappeared down the driveway.

Something was wrong. Terribly wrong. Lord Byron never acted irrationally. His keen animal instincts had alerted him to danger—a danger of which Anna Rose was unaware. But she trusted the rottweiler's innate ability to sense trouble. Her own intuition told her that someone needed her help—that out there in the dark, stormy night, a fellow human being was alone and in pain.

Without giving the weather or her own safety another thought, Anna Rose rushed back inside her warm, dry home. Reaching into the hall closet, she grabbed her raincoat and cap. Slipping the tan, water-resistant jacket over her shirt and jeans, she fastened the top two buttons, then settled the wool-felt beret on her head, pulling down one side so that it almost covered her eye. She jerked her purse off the shelf and dug inside for her keys.

Once outside, she quickly became drenched, damp strands of wispy hair clinging to her face, the wetness adding weight to the already heavy braid that hung down her back. As she ran toward the driveway, she sidestepped several deep puddles of muddy water, only to lose her footing and step directly into one of the deepest holes. Water covered her foot and wet her jeans to mid-calf. Inside her leather sneaker and squishy sock, Anna Rose flexed her toes.

She jumped into her dark blue Blazer and slammed the door. Feeling her way, she inserted the key into the ignition. Within seconds after starting the motor, she backed out of her drive and searched desperately to find Lord Byron. The Blazer's bright headlights illuminated the paved road that ran north and south in front of Anna Rose's farmhouse. She had no sooner turned out of her drive than she saw her rottweiler running ahead of her, then suddenly jumping off the the road and down an embankment.

Parking the four-wheel drive on the side of the road, Anna Rose opened the door and hopped out, her feet marring up in the thick mud. Reaching inside, she picked up the flashlight lying in the back floorboard, then gave the door a hard shove with the side of her hip. Turning her attention to where Lord Byron had exited the road in such a hurry, she cast the flashlight's beam down the steep ravine. With his heavy body braced against the side of the old Chevy truck, the dog pawed at the door.

Dear God, someone had run off the road. She didn't recognize the truck, so it had to belong to a stranger. Anna Rose knew the entire populace of Cherokee and just about everybody in the surrounding areas of Mt. Hester, Margerum, and Allsboro.

Making her way cautiously down the rain-slick embankment, Anna Rose called out to Lord Byron, who was moaning plaintively. Just as she reached the bottom of the ditch, her foot caught on the far-reaching roots of a nearby tree. Trying to steady herself, she lost her balance and fell flat on her behind. Her hand holding the flashlight plunged into thick, gooey mud while the other flattened against a growth of wet moss and grass.

"Tarnation," she grumbled as she struggled to stand.

Once at the truck, she shoved Lord Byron aside. "Down, big boy. Stay." Wiping off the flashlight on her wet jeans, she cast the beam through the window and into the cab.

He was slumped over the steering wheel. A big man with a heavy dark beard and thick, tousled black hair. He was wearing jeans and a long-sleeved gray shirt. The best she could make out through the dirty widow, whoever he was, he was unconscious.

She eased the door open, but since the truck leaned slightly to the side, she found it difficult to keep the door from closing on her. Finally she crawled into the cab and allowed the door to slam behind her, shutting her inside with the stranger. She clutched the flashlight, running the bright beam slowly over the unmoving body of the man who was now only inches from her. She'd never seen him before, so if he lived hereabouts, he was a newcomer.

Reaching out, she touched his shoulder. He didn't move. She edged closer and closer until she was sitting directly beside him. She ran her fingers over his forehead and felt a sticky wetness. When she pulled her hand away, the man moaned.

Anna Rose jumped. "Are you hurt?" she asked, then cursed herself for voicing such an inane question. Of course he was hurt. He'd wrecked his truck, he was barely conscious and his forehead was bleeding.

He made no reply, not even another moan. She touched the back of his neck, her fingers encountering the overly long hair that curled about his collar. As if on cue at the touch of her hand, he moaned again, a deeper grunting sound. She didn't flinch or pull away, but allowed her hand to travel down his back and across to his shoulder, her arm draping about his massive width.

Slowly he turned his head, but didn't try to lift it from the steering wheel. He opened his eyes, gazing up at her. For one tiny instant, one delicate moment, Anna Rose looked into the stranger's topaz-flecked brown eyes and felt as if she had met her destiny. Quickly she brushed aside the foolishly romantic notion.

"It's going to be all right," she said, wanting desperately to reassure him. He kept staring at her, not moving, not speaking, just staring.

"Are you badly hurt?" she asked. The agonized look in his eyes told her that he was in great pain and yet she saw no evidence of any physical injuries other than the cut on his forehead, where the oozing blood was already beginning to congeal. "My phone's out, so there's no way I can call for an ambulance or help of any kind."

When he closed his eyes, Anna Rose felt an irrational fear surge through her. This man couldn't die. He couldn't! She didn't understand why her concern for this stranger was more than one human being's care for another, but it was.

"We've got to get you out of here," she told him, squeezing his shoulder. "Do you think you can help?"

He opened his eyes again, lifting his head slightly and turning to face her. Inside the darkness of the truck cab, the only illumination came from the small flashlight Anna Rose still held in her hand.

"Get that damned light out of my eyes." His voice was a deep, deadly rumble.

Anna Rose gulped in surprise, heat rising to her face. Shocked by his angry command, she didn't immediately remove the source of his irritation, allowing the light to remain on his face long enough to make a thorough inspection of his hairy appearance. He wasn't handsome, but he was totally masculine. And he was badly scarred, at least on the left side of his face and neck. The heavy beard and mustache concealed a great deal of the scarring, but not across his forehead or along the flesh exposed by the open collar of his shirt.

A sudden chill racked her body. She wasn't repulsed by the man's scars. She was deeply saddened. What pain he must have known, must still endure, if no longer physical, then emotional. Instinctively she knew the agony she'd seen in his eyes only moments ago came from the past, not the present.

Realizing that she hadn't moved the flashlight, she turned it off and stuck it in her pocket. "Do you think you can walk?"

"I can try." He raised his head and leaned back against the seat, trapping Anna Rose's arm.

She slipped her arm out from beneath his broad shoulders. "My Blazer is parked up on the road. It's a steep climb and the ground is slick from all the rain."

"Were you driving along and saw the truck down here?" he asked, running his big hands over his face, as if trying to awaken himself from a bad dream.

"No, I live back off the road a piece. My dog heard something and I followed him." She thought it rather odd that she and a perfect stranger were sitting inside his wrecked truck having a normal conversation while outside the wind and rain ravaged the earth, and Lord Byron howled as he pawed at the door.

The man moved, brushing up against her. She stared at him, open-mouthed and wide-eyed. "I can't get out of the truck until you do," he said. "This door is jammed against the side of the embankment." He nodded toward the driver's side of the truck.

Hurriedly Anna Rose slid across the seat and opened the door. The rain blew inside. The strong wind fought with her as she struggled to keep the door open. He reached across her, bracing the door with his powerful hand while she stepped out of the truck. She turned to assist him, but he brushed her hands away, stepped out and grabbed the rim of the truck bed to brace his unsteady legs.

"Don't try to be so macho." She slipped her arm around his waist. "Lean on me. I'm not some fragile little female who's going to break in two."

She felt his compliance, and wondered if she had spoken too hastily. Merciful heavens, he was heavy. And tall. She wasn't short herself, standing five-foot-nine in her bare feet, but this man towered over her a good five or six inches.

"I'm too heavy," he said, easing away from her. "I'm hurting you."

She tightened her hold about his waist, refusing to release him. "Don't be an idiot. You can't make it up to the road without help."

Off in the distance, a low roll of thunder sounded, followed by a brilliant flash of lightning that momentarily illuminated their faces. She noted a spark of amusement in his eyes while he saw the look of determination in hers.

"Are you by any chance a marine corps drill instructor?" he asked as she guided him toward the steep incline of slippery rocks, mud and grass.

"Very funny." She felt her feet mar up in the mud. They seemed to have heavy weights attached, slowing her progress. And it didn't help that the man at her side halted momentarily. "Don't you dare pass out. It's not much farther. Just hang on."

"You're a prison warden?" He held on to her, following her lead as she guided him onward and upward toward the road.

"You have a very warped sense of humor. Here I am trying to rescue you and all you can do is insult me." She was beginning to wonder if she were dreaming all this and that any minute she'd awaken to find herself all warm and dry inside her house.

Finally they reached the top of the embankment. The bright glare from the Blazer's headlights struck them boldly as they moved along the roadside. Lord Byron followed, and when Anna Rose opened the passenger door, the dog, all muddy feet and dripping wet fur, jumped in the back seat.

"Tarnation, Lord Byron. Double, triple tarnation. I ought to paddle your backside." She stood beside the open door, hands on her hips, the wind whipping loose strands of hair into her mouth as she scolded her disobedient pet. A slow, steady rainfall pelted her robust body.

Britt Cameron watched her, wondering what the hell it was about this strange woman that amused him so much. He'd known her for all of ten minutes and she'd already made him smile more than he'd smiled in a couple of years. "I've got it," he said. "You're a schoolteacher."

She turned, giving him a startled then condemning look. "Get in. I'll take you back to the house with me. The phone was out when I left, but we'll check and see of it's working now."

Man, she was bossy, he thought. As bossy as his mother. Maybe that was the reason he liked her, the reason he didn't feel threatened by the fact that she was a woman. She re-

minded him of his mother. Hell, how could a woman like
that give him any trouble?

"Yes, ma'am." He got inside, slammed the door and
watched while she circled the vehicle, getting in on the other
side.

Suddenly he felt the nuzzle of the rottweiler's damp nose
against his shoulder. Turning slightly, he came face-to-face
with the biggest dog he'd ever seen. "Does he bite?" Britt
asked.

Anna Rose started the Blazer and began backing up.
"Only if I tell him to." Even in the darkness, Britt knew she
was smiling—could almost see the corners of her wide, full
mouth turning up.

He was surprised at how well she maneuvered the four-
wheel drive on the dark country road in a storm, and how
unemotionally she had handled his rescue from the truck.
She wasn't like the women he'd known, certainly nothing
like the type of woman he preferred—petite and blonde and
utterly feminine in their helplessness. Tanya had been like
that. Tanya, the girl he'd adored since childhood. The girl
who'd married his best friend and who had been widowed
at twenty-two when Paul had died in the accident that, even
now, Britt blamed on himself.

"If the phone's still out, you'll be stuck here till morning." Anna Rose pulled the Blazer into the drive beside her
house.

"Why can't you take me into the nearest town for a
wrecker?" he asked.

"The road into town is flooded. That happens whenever
it rains a lot. The only way out would be back the way you
came."

"I see." He had no intention of going back to Mississippi. Certainly not tonight or tomorrow. Not for a long,
long time.

"Can you make a dash for the house or do you need
help?" She shut off the motor and turned toward him,

sensing more than seeing his large hulking frame in the darkness.

"I think I can make it."

"Wait until I get to the house." Without hesitation she flung open the door on the driver's side, jumped out, then waited a couple of seconds for Lord Byron to hurl himself over the seat and into the yard before she slammed the door.

Britt could barely see the house, so he waited as long as he thought it would take for her to get inside before he threw open the door and made a mad dash up the front steps.

She stood in the doorway, a soft rosy light illuminating the entrance. She looked like a very large drowned rat, he thought. When he stepped over the threshold and entered the warm, dry hallway, he felt a sudden sense of peace—almost of homecoming. When he shook his head to dislodge such ridiculous notions, droplets of moisture jetted off his hair. Realizing he was making a muddy mess in her foyer, he started to apologize when he noticed that Lord Byron was shaking off far more water and had left wet, dirty paw prints on the wooden floor.

He watched while she removed her raincoat and beret and hung them in the hall closet. Underneath she wore a large, billowy blouse. He thought it looked like a man's shirt. Her jeans were baggy, damp all over and soaking wet from the knees down. He wasn't certain if she was a bit on the plump side or if a trim figure was hidden beneath the overly loose clothing.

Anna Rose caught him giving her a thorough appraisal and had the oddest feeling, as if she should try to cover herself because this man could see straight through her clothes. What a silly thought, she told herself.

"Look, just go into the living room. I'm going to get out of these wet clothes and I'll see if I can't find something of my grandfather's that will fit you." She smiled at him and was disappointed when he didn't return the smile.

"You live here with your grandfather?" he asked, glancing around the hallway and through the open door into the the dark living room.

"He died several years ago. I live here alone, except for Lord Byron and a few stray animals that come and go." She picked up the kerosene lamp from the hall tree and handed it to him.

"Won't you need this to see where you're going?" Their hands touched briefly when the lamp went from her possession into his.

She couldn't help but notice his left hand. It was all she could do to stop herself from gasping out loud. The skin was badly scarred, obviously from a severe wound, and two fingers were twined together like knotted tree roots.

"There's another lamp lit in my bedroom." She nodded down the hall and to the right, praying that he hadn't noticed the shock on her face or the slight hesitation in her voice.

When she started to walk away, he reached out and touched her on the shoulder with his crippled hand. "Aren't you afraid to be alone in your home with a stranger? For all you know I could be some maniac, an escapee from the looney bin . . . a murderer."

"I'm Anna Rose Palmer," she said. "Introduce yourself and we won't be strangers."

There it was again, he thought. That irresistible urge to laugh. But he didn't even smile, except inside his mind. "Britt Cameron." He watched her closely for a reaction. After all, he couldn't be more than forty or fifty miles outside Riverton. It was possible that she'd heard about the trial.

"Pleased to meet you, Britt Cameron." Her gaze traveled over him slowly, measuring him up the way he'd assessed her a few minutes ago. "When I helped you up out of the ditch, I didn't see or feel any weapons on you. No gun or knife. So unless you can figure out some way to kill Lord

Byron with your bare hands, there's no way he'll allow you to hurt me.''

Britt was glad she hadn't recognized his name, relieved that he wouldn't be sent back out into the dark, rainy night . . . alone. ''I promise to be on my best behavior.'' He turned and went into the living room.

Anna Rose rushed down the hall and into her bedroom. With nervous fingers, she removed her soggy shoes and socks, then stripped out of her wet clothes and slipped into a fresh pair of slacks and an oversize cotton sweater. All the while she was unbraiding her damp hair, she kept thinking about the man in her living room—the man who had wrecked his truck in front of her house. She didn't think he'd been drinking. She hadn't smelled anything on his breath, and they'd been close enough that their lips could have touched if either of them had moved a fraction closer.

She picked up the kerosene lamp from her nightstand and went into the bedroom that had once belonged to her grandparents. It had remained unchanged since her childhood. As she searched through the contents of the cedar chest that sat at the foot of the bed, she wondered about Britt Cameron. Odd—wasn't it?—that she'd been thinking about needing a temporary man in her life, someone she could pass off as her mystery fiancé, and then, *poof,* out of nowhere, a tall, dark stranger had appeared.

''I hope these fit,'' she said aloud as she pulled out a pair of faded jeans and a khaki, cotton work shirt. Gramps had been a big man, probably a bit heavier than Britt Cameron, but Anna Rose didn't think he'd been quite as tall. Oh, well, these clothes would just have to do until her houseguest's own clothes dried.

Feeling her way more than seeing, she made a quick stop by the bathroom before going back up the hall. She found Britt standing at the windows, watching the storm outside. The minute she entered the living room, he turned and faced her.

He noticed that she had her arms full. Sitting atop a pile of clothes was what appeared to be a first-aid kit. "Can I help you with some of that?"

She laid the kit on the sofa beside her book of poetry, then handed him Gramps's old clothes. "You can change in here. I'll go in the kitchen and fix us some coffee." She took several tentative steps, then stopped. "Are you hungry?" she asked. "I could fix you a sandwich or...I've got some cold fried chicken."

"Thanks. A sandwich would be great." He'd never met a woman like Anna Rose Palmer. She seemed to be bossy and independent and yet at the same time she possessed an old-fashioned sense of hospitality and friendliness. He couldn't figure her out.

"I'll knock before I come back in here. Feel free to check the phone, but I doubt it's working. We've had rain for over a week and the phone's been out for a couple of days. The roads are in a terrible mess. I barely made it home from school this afternoon."

"You *are* a schoolteacher." He smiled then, despite all his efforts not to. He didn't want to like this woman. Hell, he never wanted to like another woman as long as he lived. But Anna Rose didn't pose a threat to him. He wasn't attracted to her. Not that way. She was tall and plump and rather plain. And bossier than his mother. Good God, there was no way he could ever be physically attracted to a woman like that.

"I'm the principal of Cherokee's elementary school." She liked his smile. It softened his harsh face and put a warm sparkle in his sad topaz eyes. "Change clothes. Just lay your wet things in the hall. I'll have you some coffee and a sandwich ready in a few minutes."

"How about some coffee first?" He could use something warm in his stomach. The rain had drenched him down to his briefs, chilling him to the bone.

"Sure thing."

"Won't you need the lamp?" he asked.

"You'll need it. I can feel my way, then light a couple of candles I keep on the kitchen counter for occasions like this."

Britt took his time stripping. He noticed she hadn't bothered to bring him any underwear. It didn't make any difference. He'd just do without. He had no intention of wearing his soaked briefs. The clothes were old, faded and a bit worn, but damn comfortable. The shirt was a fairly good fit, but the pants were a couple of inches too short and at least three inches too big in the waist. He looped his own belt through the loose jeans.

Should I tell her who I am? he wondered. *She has a right to know that I was an accused murderer and that half my hometown still thinks I killed my wife.*

He hadn't murdered Tanya. Hell, he'd loved the girl . . . loved her since they'd been kids when she'd tagged along after him and Paul. But she'd never loved him as anything but a friend, even though she'd married him after Paul's death. No, Tanya had never loved anyone but Paul Rogers. Certainly not that pretty-boy minister, Timothy Charles—the guy she'd run off with six months before her death.

A loud knock on the door brought Britt back from thoughts of the past. "Come on in," he said. "I'm decent."

Anna Rose eyed her guest, then smiled at the way he looked in Gramps's clothes. "Oh, my. I was afraid the pants wouldn't fit. Come on over here and sit down on the couch and drink your coffee while I clean that cut on your head."

"Ms. Palmer, are you always so bossy?" Although he questioned her orders, he followed them, seating himself on the large, colorful sofa.

"Bossiness is one of my many shortcomings. And call me Anna Rose." Seating herself beside Britt, she handed him the mug of steaming black coffee. "No sugar or cream."

He nodded that she had guessed his preference correctly.

Placing her book on an end table and the first-aid kit in her lap, she ran her fingers through his hair, pulling the long, damp strands off his forehead. "Doesn't look like more than a scratch, but you've got a nasty bruise. Weren't you wearing your seat belt?"

"My truck is a classic and not equipped with seat belts." He studied her while she cleaned his wound. Her eyes were a very dark blue. Like sapphires, he thought, then wondered where that comparison had come from.

"What happened?" she asked, replacing everything in the kit. "Were you driving too fast and just lost control?"

"Nope. I was creeping along. Couldn't see more than a few feet in front of me. A deer dashed across the road. I missed the deer, but hit a wet spot and skidded into the ditch."

"Well, this far out, you're likely to see deer crossing the road pretty often. There's a hunting lodge a few miles from here." She watched as he raised the mug to his lips and drank, slowly but steadily.

"Good coffee. Thanks."

"You're welcome." She couldn't seem to pull her gaze away from his left hand. What on earth could have happened? Surely the doctors could repair it, could do plastic surgery and remove the scars on his face and neck. Why would a man as young and vitally attractive leave such reminders of an experience that must have been agonizingly painful? She longed to ask him, longed to tell him that he could share his pain with her, that she understood the loneliness she saw in his eyes.

Britt tried not to let the way she was staring at his hand bother him. Tightening the hold on the mug, he averted her questioning eyes. He knew she was wondering what had happened to him. Was she feeling sorry for him? Or was she simply repulsed by the sight of his scars and deformed hand?

He could have had the scars removed, even allowed the doctors to perform some experimental surgery in the hopes of partially restoring life back into his useless fingers. But he didn't want the reminders erased. Paul had died in the accident, and he had lived. He'd been driving. Too fast, maybe, even though the police said the accident had been no one's fault. A tire had blown. The car had swerved and hit a tree, then exploded into flames. He'd been thrown free. Paul had been trapped inside. He'd received the burns, the damage to his hand when he'd tried to rescue Paul. He'd passed out from the pain, and Paul had burned to death. He would never forget. And he would never forgive himself.

Anna Rose knew that he'd noticed her staring at his hand. She'd seen the pain, the anger, and then the glazed look of a man remembering...remembering something that haunted him.

"I'll go fix that sandwich for you now," she said. "Make yourself at home. I'll prepare a bed for you after you eat."

She couldn't get out of the living room fast enough. She had to get away from Britt Cameron, away from her overwhelming need to comfort him. Her feminine instincts told her that he wouldn't welcome her pity or her comfort.

Britt finished his coffee, set the cup on the end table and stretched out on the big, comfortable sofa. The soft, golden glow from the lone kerosene lamp cast flickering shadows across the room. It was a warm, welcoming room, he thought. A room filled with contentment. Anna Rose Palmer reminded him of just such an emotion. Contentment. She was the kind of woman that made a man feel comfortable. The kind of woman a man could talk to, share things with. A strong woman a man could lean on if he needed to.

"Hell, Cameron, what's the matter with you? You'll be leaving here in the morning and you'll never see the woman again."

A few minutes later Anna Rose came back into the living room carrying a tray. She'd fixed him a chicken sandwich, thick and piled high with sliced meat, tomatoes and lettuce. She'd opened a bag of potato chips, poured him a fresh cup of coffee and added one of her homemade dill pickles to his plate.

"Here we are," she said, then hushed immediately when she saw his big body lying on the sofa, his eyes closed and his breathing deep and even. He was asleep.

Setting the tray on the library table, she gazed down at Britt Cameron. He didn't look quite as ferocious, quite as threatening, asleep, she thought, then trembled when she realized that, subconsciously, she'd been thinking of this man as dangerous. But sleep took nothing away from his size, the breadth of his shoulders, the hard muscles in his arms and long legs. Nor did sleep diminish his dark, mysterious looks.

Anna Rose picked up a hand-crocheted afghan and laid it over Britt. Even though it was late May in Alabama, the nights after a heavy rain could still be chilly. Without thinking, she ran her fingers across the scars on his forehead. When he grunted, she jerked her hand away.

Before leaving, she took one last look. "Well, Lord," she whispered. "I prayed for a man, but I'm afraid you might have given me just a little bit more than I can handle."

Two

Anna Rose awoke at a little after six. Years of getting up early had set her internal clock and it refused to allow her extra sleep even on weekends. She sat up in the half-canopy bed that had been passed down in the Palmer family for generations. The ornately carved mahogany bed matched the chest and armoire that decorated her room, a room that looked as if it had been plucked from the pages of history. Anna Rose loved the antiques that filled her home, and she cared for them with adoration and pride.

She noticed bright sunshine pushing against the curtained windows and French door, seeping through the fabric and around the corners to lighten the cool darkness inside. A soft morning breeze was blowing. She could hear the gentle scrape of the weeping willow branches against the side of the house.

Stretching her arms over her head, she sighed, feeling an undeniable soreness in her limbs and back. Helping Britt Cameron climb the steep embankment onto the road had exercised unused muscles, leaving her body aching. Wondering how her visitor had fared the night, she got out of bed, slipping on her floor-length cotton robe over her gown. If she hurried, she might have breakfast finished before he awoke. The thought of sharing breakfast with a man gave Anna Rose a rush of delight.

She opened her bedroom door and stepped into the hall. Just as she was chastising herself for being a silly romantic fool, Britt walked out of the bathroom across the corridor. She opened her mouth on a startled gasp, then sucked in an awed breath. He stood only a few feet from her, tall and dark and overwhelmingly big, wearing nothing but her grandfather's too short jeans.

Although she'd seen men in shorts and swim trunks, she'd never realized how erotic a man's partially naked body could be, but then, few men looked like Britt Cameron. His black hair was worn a bit too long for fashion. Thick and wavy, it curled about his neck and a few loose strands fell across his forehead. His heavy beard and mustache gave him a look of mystery, the appearance of a rugged warrior, of a saddle-weary cowboy, of a ruthless pirate.

"Good...good morning." She forced the words, her breath caught in her lungs, creating an ache in her chest.

"Morning." He didn't move. He simply stared back at her.

Anna Rose tried to stop looking at him, but seemed powerless to end her perusal of his totally male physique. His shoulders were unbelievably broad and sculptured with large, smooth muscles. His big arms were covered with a smattering of dark hair, as was his thick chest, where a dense swirl of blackness centered between his bulging pectoral muscles and arrowed down his belly and into his jeans.

In the dimly lit hallway, the scars that marred his otherwise perfect appearance took little away from his devastatingly masculine appeal—indeed their very existence seemed to add to his powerful macho aura.

"I hope it's all right that I went ahead and took a shower," he said, noting the oddly dazed look in her eyes, the peculiar way she was staring at him. "I tried the phone already. It's still out."

"Oh ... I—I'm not surprised." She willed herself to act rationally, not like some sex-starved old maid. Tarnation, how she hated that term—*old maid*. It was an antiquated term, but one still widely used in the rural South, and most definitely overused in Cherokee, Alabama.

"Thanks for drying my clothes." He plunged his hands into his pockets, the gesture tugging on the overly loose waistband and lowering it to hip level. "I found them on the rocking chair in the living room. I was just fixing to put them on."

She swallowed—swallowed hard. His hips were lean and narrow. She couldn't take her eyes off that line of black hair that thickened at his navel. "You're welcome," she gulped the words.

"Do you suppose the road is clear so you can take me into town for a wrecker?" he asked, his gaze traveling leisurely over her sleep-tousled appearance. In the soft lighting, she was almost pretty, a fact he tried to dismiss from his mind.

"If it's still flooded, I can drive you back into Mississippi to the first town over the state line, or we can go the long way around into Cherokee. It'll take forever."

Britt's attention was caught by the way her breasts lifted when she breathed deeply, as if she were nervous and trying desperately to calm herself. Her faded housecoat hung open from shoulders to hem, and her thin, slightly worn cotton gown did little to conceal the lush fullness of her breasts or the curve of her wide hips and the shadowed cleft between her long legs.

Unwanted and completely unexpected, Britt's body responded in a natural way to the feminine allure of the woman standing so close to him. He cursed his arousal, and since he didn't find her attractive, he couldn't understand his reaction.

"Won't you stay for breakfast?" she asked, hoping beyond hope that he would stay.

"Sure . . . sure. Breakfast would be nice. If it wouldn't be too much trouble." He looked directly at her. That was a mistake. There was something gentle, almost lovely about her features. The wide mouth and full lips. The long, slightly large nose. The heavy-lidded, sapphire-blue eyes. And a mane of ash-brown hair that hung over her shoulders and down her back halfway to her waist. Britt's body tightened, his masculinity threatening to embarrass him. Luckily she didn't seem to notice his blatant state of arousal.

"You can change clothes, then go out back to the patio. I'll get dressed and fix breakfast and we'll eat outside." She had always dreamed of sharing breakfast on the rock patio with a man—a special man with whom she'd shared an unforgettable night. Well, she laughed to herself, she most certainly would never forget last night.

"Yeah, well . . . yeah. Fine." With his hands still in his pockets, he turned and went down the hall, grateful that Anna Rose Palmer had either not noticed his condition or was too much of a lady to mention it.

He swept the fallen leaves, small sticks and pieces of debris from the patio, all the while breathing in the fresh, after-rain smell of the world, and occasionally stealing glances at Anna Rose as she dried off the wooden table and chairs with a ragged towel. She had changed out of her revealing nightgown into some rather dowdy, beige twill slacks and a long-sleeved white blouse that hung below her hips. She'd pulled her hair into a loose ponytail, and not a smidgen of makeup adorned her pale face or covered the delicate splattering of freckles across her nose.

"Isn't everything beautiful after a rain?" She hugged her arms tightly across her chest as she looked up at the sky. "So fresh and clean. Almost new."

"Yeah. Like the world's starting all over." He watched her, noting the way she seemed to absorb the simple beauty of the day into her, as if she were able to draw strength from the natural wonders surrounding her. She's like this morning, he thought. Anna Rose is fresh and clean. He knew nothing about her life, and yet whatever she had experienced hadn't erased the facade of innocence she projected.

"Breakfast will be ready as soon as the biscuits are done," she told him. "I'll set the table."

When she turned to go back inside the house, he called out, "Where's Lord Byron this morning?"

"Oh, he ate in the kitchen and now he's out exploring in the woods with CoCo and Snowball."

"Friends of his?"

"They're a couple of strays that I've been feeding."

Britt sat down in one of the enormous redwood chairs, stretching his long legs out and crossing them at the ankles. Anna Rose's house reminded him a lot of home, now that his brother Wade's wife Lydia had redecorated the run-down Victorian structure. The furniture at home was mostly new, except for the few antique pieces Lydia had found at estate sales. But Anna Rose's well-kept house was filled with old furniture, polished to a gleaming shine. Her yard was neatly manicured, spring flowers blooming in abundance, their rain-and-wind-battered petals strewn hither and yon.

From the patio he could see endless acres of land, cultivated crops as far as the eye could see to the north and south on each side of the house and verdant forest to the west behind the house. The house itself, painted a pristine white, boasted a dark green roof and matching shutters. Delicately carved gingerbread trim created a fancy lace edging on the two-story structure and the one small third-story turret room.

Anna Rose returned with blue gingham place mats, matching napkins and glistening silverware. "The biscuits are ready." She smiled at him when he turned to face her. "I have homemade strawberry jam, pear preserves and grape jelly. Which do you prefer?"

"Pear preserves." Ma always canned several extra pints for him every year. They were his favorite. Nothing tasted quite as good on hot buttered biscuits. Although she'd been raised in the country, Tanya had never learned how to can fresh fruits and vegetables.

"I'll be right back," Anna Rose said.

"Need any help?"

"No, thanks. I've got everything on a serving cart."

He looked at the neat, homey setting she'd spread out on the redwood picnic table. All it needed, besides food, to be perfect was a bouquet of flowers in the center. Wade's wife Lydia loved flowers, and had filled the old homeplace with them after she'd redecorated and made the house truly hers. Britt figured Anna Rose probably liked flowers as much as Lydia did. Maybe it was a female thing. Without thinking, he got up, walked into the yard and began searching. Finally, near the barn he saw something that looked like white daisies growing in profusion. After picking a handful of the wildflowers, he started back toward the patio.

Anna Rose rolled a wooden cart filled with food to the table, looked around in search of Britt, and sighed with relief when she saw him coming toward her. Narrowing her eyes, she squinted against the hazy sunshine and tried to figure out what he carried in one hand. When he neared, she realized that he held a huge bouquet of daisies.

She stood there staring at him, smiling back and forth from him to the flowers. He shifted uncomfortably and grunted. "You fixed everything up so fancy, I thought you'd probably want a centerpiece." Damn, he felt like an idiot. What the hell had prompted him to go running off to pick flowers? He'd never done anything so... so unmanly in all his life.

"Oh, Britt, what a sweet thought." She reached out and took the bouquet when he thrust it at her. "They're beautiful. Sit down and eat. I'll go put these in a vase and be right back."

"Hey, there's no need—" He tried to tell her that she didn't need to stick the damn weeds in a vase. They weren't anything but wildflowers. They were more suited to being stuck in a tin can, he thought. But before he could protest, she whirled around and went back inside.

His feelings of discomfort soon vanished when he sat down at the table and breathed in the succulent aroma of ham and redeye gravy, scrambled eggs, crisp hash browns and hot coffee. If everything tasted half as good as it looked, Anna Rose Palmer was a whiz in the kitchen. He picked up the china cup, noting the blue flowered pattern just as his lips touched the rim. Delicious. The best damn coffee he'd ever drunk. Even better than Ma's, and that was saying a lot.

Savoring the heavenly taste of the morning's first cup of coffee, he glanced up to see Anna Rose bending over and placing the vase of daises in the center of the table. The vase matched the dishes—a crisp white, edged with tiny blue flowers.

"This is just perfect," she said as she sat down across from him.

Her face glowed with health and vitality and some inner happiness he didn't even try to discern. In the brutal light of day, he couldn't help but notice that Anna Rose was no great beauty. Her features were too strong, too vibrant. And yet, that very strength plus the Amazon proportions of her body combined to make a rather striking woman. But, dear God, her taste in clothes was awful. He wondered if she had anything in her wardrobe that actually fit her body, or if all her attire had been purchased at least one size larger than she needed.

"Eat up," she told him. "Enjoy everything while it's hot." She began by breaking open a fluffy biscuit and spreading a thick layer of pear preserves on each half.

For several minutes they each ate in silence. Britt thought that if the way to a man's heart was through his stomach,

Anna Rose Palmer would have men lined up from her front porch into the next county.

"More coffee?" she asked, and, when he nodded, she poured from the sterling-silver pot.

Amazed by her healthy appetite, he thought about the other women he'd known over the years. None of them would have indulged in eating so heartily in front of a man they barely knew. As a matter of fact, most women of his acquaintance were always dieting. "How much of this land belongs to you?" he asked, nodding his head from left to right.

"About five hundred acres altogether." She finished off her second cup of coffee and poured a third, lacing it liberally with cream and sugar.

"You don't farm it yourself, do you?"

"I rent out some of it, but there are acres just sitting idle since Gramps died. A place this size needs a full-time farmer and I'm afraid my job in town pretty well fills my life." She thought about the offers she'd had for her land, and knew she'd never sell. She didn't need the money. Her salary was sufficient for her needs and what she collected in rent more than covered the cost of upkeep on the house and the farm itself. No, this land had been in her family since before the Civil War, and someday, God willing, she'd pass it down to her own children.

"I grew up on a farm something like this." He sipped his coffee as he leaned back in the redwood chair. It had been a long time since he'd enjoyed a meal so much.

"Is there . . . someone . . . anyone that you need to call? I mean is there someone who'd be worried about you?" What if Britt were married? she thought. It would be impossible to ask a married man to pose as her fiancé.

"My folks aren't expecting me back for a while." His conscience urged him to tell her the truth. After all, didn't her generous hospitality afford her that much?

"No wife and children?" she asked, not caring if he might take her inquisition the wrong way.

"I've never had a child...and I don't have a wife." He had wanted children, longed to see Tanya pregnant, had hoped a baby would save their doomed marriage. But she hadn't wanted a child. Not his, anyway.

The poignantly sweet smell of honeysuckle wafted through the mild spring breeze while Anna Rose sat on her patio sharing a fantasy breakfast with an unmarried man who just might be the answer to her prayers. If only there was some way to persuade Britt Cameron to hang around a few more days, she could tell everyone that he was her fiancé. Then when he left, she'd simply explain that they'd had a quarrel and had broken the engagement. There was no reason why anyone had to know the truth about her foolish lie.

While they continued enjoying the peaceful morning and savoring the last of the fresh coffee, Anna Rose studied Britt as discreetly as possible. Through most of the meal, he'd seemed peaceful and relaxed, as if he were thoroughly enjoying himself. But when she'd asked him about a wife and children, his mood had altered. After responding to her question, he'd become quiet and withdrawn, and she'd felt a deep sorrow within him. It made her want to reach out and put her arms around him. Instinctively knowing he needed comfort, she longed to share his pain, ease his loneliness with all the stored-up love in her heart.

But Britt didn't look like a man who'd readily accept a woman's tenderness. Certainly not from her, a plain Jane whose forceful personality kept most men at arm's length.

In the bright, clear light of day, Britt's scars were vividly apparent. Puckered burn scars spread in thin, prominent lines across the left side of his forehead and into the density of his dark beard. Along his neck the scarring grew wider. Remembering him without a shirt, she knew the scars tapered off into nothingness as they approached his left arm.

She watched while he clutched the delicate china cup with his right hand, totally encompassing it. His left hand, which she'd noticed he seldom used, lay in his lap. She wondered again, what horrible event had marred this man for life, and why with the miracles of modern medicine he hadn't undergone reconstructive surgery. Then, perhaps he had, she thought. No, surely not. Unless . . .

Two tiny brown sparrows played in a nearby puddle of standing rainwater, dipping low, flapping their wings, relishing in the cleansing spray from their private pool. In three backyard trees, wooden bird feeders swayed in the breeze, and a lone gray squirrel scurried about from branch to branch, springing effortlessly from tree to tree like an accomplished highwire performer.

"Do you need a job?" she asked.

Snapping his head around, Britt glared at her, uncertain he'd heard her question correctly. "What?"

Anna Rose's cheeks flushed with embarrassment. She hadn't meant to blurt out her offer without some preamble, but, as usual, her forthright manner had taken precedence over better judgment. "I'm sorry. I should explain. You see, Corey Randall, my sort of . . . well, handyman around the place, had an accident and broke his leg several days ago."

"Handyman, huh?"

"Well, he keeps the house, the yard, the barn in good repair. Also, he checks the fences, makes sure no one is on my land without permission. Those sorts of things." She couldn't tell by the blank expression on Britt's face what his reaction was to her explanation.

"Are you offering me the job?" he asked, his topaz eyes narrowing to oval slits.

"Yes, on a temporary basis. The doctor said Corey probably wouldn't be able to work for about six weeks."

"Six weeks?" He ran his fingers over the short, neatly trimmed beard that spread across his chin and jawline. "How much does it pay?"

"The pay is minimum wage, but I could throw in room and board."

"You'd want me to stay here, with you?" He gave her an amused look.

"No, of course not." She emitted an exasperated huff. "There's an old sharecropper's shack about a quarter of a mile down the road. You'd need to clean it up and air it out, but it has electricity, indoor plumbing and the essentials in furniture. Bed, chairs, stuff like that."

"You'd provide groceries or would I take my meals with you?"

"The shack doesn't have a stove, just an old hot plate...no real kitchen. You'd have to come up to the house for meals." She desperately wanted him to take this job. His presence around the farm, even for a few weeks, could solve her mystery fiancé problem. "There's no air-conditioning, but the job won't last into much of July, and the house is in a grove of trees."

Britt didn't know why her offer was so appealing, why he was even considering accepting it. "How do you know you can trust me? What makes you so sure I'm not just some shiftless, lazy bum?"

"Instinct tells me you're trustworthy. And if you don't earn your salary, I'll fire you." She didn't want to sound too eager, push too hard, but she uttered up a silent prayer that he would accept her offer. She told herself that she simply needed his assistance to get herself out of a sticky social situation. Although the thought that she was taking in yet another stray, hoping to the heal the wounds of one more of God's injured creatures appealed to her sense of reason, she refused to acknowledge the way Britt Cameron made her feel every time she looked at him.

Britt considered his options. He was a man with no place to go...a man who badly needed a sanctuary, a place to hide away and lick his wounds. Anna Rose didn't know who he was, had no idea the trauma he'd lived through. Should he tell her? Did he dare to be totally honest with her? "I can't promise I'll stay the entire six weeks," he said, his gaze meeting hers. "Would you hire me on a week-to-week basis?"

Obviously he didn't want to be committed. Whatever he was running from, he wanted to be able to flee again if it caught up with him. Anna Rose knew she would take him on any terms. "Today's Saturday. How about a Saturday-to-Saturday basis?"

"Deal," he said.

"Deal." She smiled, certain that Britt Cameron's arrival the night before hadn't been a mere accident. He'd been sent to her—a gift from on high.

He stuck out his right hand. She accepted his strong, brisk handshake. The touch of his flesh against hers shook her slightly, giving her a breathless, nervous feeling. She hoped he hadn't noticed how she'd quivered just as he'd pulled his hand away.

"Why don't you take a look around the place while I clean up these dishes?" She began clearing away the table, stacking everything onto the cart. "Check out the barn. I don't have any cattle or horses now, but I expect you to keep it clean. The barn's open to stray animals. Dogs, cats, any animal in need of some food and a dry place to sleep."

Britt stood, then set his empty plate and cup on the cart. "You sound like my sister, Lily. She was always bringing home strays. Biggest fool over animals I ever saw."

Anna Rose laughed, and the sweet, honest sound touched Britt, making him want to respond in kind. He didn't like the idea that he was enjoying a woman's company. But what harm could this woman's presence cause him? Her plain looks didn't tempt him, and her bossiness certainly wasn't an inducement. And somehow he knew she wasn't the nosy kind, so she wouldn't be prying into his life, trying to discover his secrets. No, Anna Rose was the type of woman who'd leave a man alone.

"Need some help with these dishes?" he asked.

"You mean you're not too macho to do dishes?"

"Around our house, chores were chores. My brother and I mopped floors, washed dishes and made beds just like our sisters, and they had to milk cows, drive a tractor and pitch hay. Believe me, Ruthie Cameron was an equal opportunity mother. She made all four of her children, regardless of sex, work their butts off."

"I like your mother."

"She'd like you," he said without thinking. But it was true. He wondered if everyone liked Anna Rose. She seemed to be the kind of person who could easily endear herself to others. He certainly liked her, despite trying so hard not to.

"You go on and look around. I'll take you over so you can see the sharecropper shack in a little while, then we'll find some way to get to a garage. You'll need your truck. I let Corey keep the farm truck. He doesn't own a vehicle of his own."

Fifteen minutes later, Britt decided that running his truck into a ditch in front of Anna Rose Palmer's house had been a blessing in disguise. Her job offered him a temporary safe haven from the world, from his overly compassionate family, from the vicious suspicions that bombarded him in Riverton, and, if he were lucky, he would stay busy enough to keep the memories at bay.

He felt guilty for not telling Anna Rose that he'd been an accused murderer, only yesterday acquitted of a crime he had not committed. Oh, there had been a time when he'd wanted to kill Tanya. Hell, he'd spouted off for weeks after she left him, telling anyone who'd listen that if she and that holier-than-thou minister ever showed their faces back in Riverton, he'd kill them both. But by the time Tanya had come back, he hadn't wanted to harm her. He hadn't even wanted to see her.

He couldn't remember a time in his life when he hadn't loved Tanya. Ever since they'd been kids. But she'd never seen him as anything but a friend. She'd loved Paul, had married Paul, and had been pregnant with Paul's baby when . . .

Damn, he'd been a fool to marry her knowing she was still in love with her dead husband. But after Paul's death and her miscarriage, Tanya had tried to commit suicide. He had wanted to give her a reason to live, and had, stupidly, thought that offering her a new life with him would make her as happy as it did him. But his happiness had been short-lived. Their two-year marriage had been a disaster.

In retrospect, he couldn't blame Tanya. He'd practically forced her into the marriage. It hadn't been her fault that desperation drove her away, that she turned to the most sympathetic man in town—Reverend Timothy Charles. Young, handsome, charismatic. A man who, even after having committed adultery, had been forgiven by the people of Riverton, while those same people, unjustly, condemned Britt as a murderer.

If he'd thought for one minute he could have proven them wrong, he'd have stayed in Riverton. But what difference did it make? His own life wasn't worth a damn and neither was his reputation. Besides, he had no proof to substantiate his suspicions, and not even Sheriff Leonard Jett, who'd known Britt all his life, would listen to his accusations when he'd tried to tell Jett that he knew who had really killed Tanya. Hell, his own mother had looked at him with shocked disbelief when he'd told her that he thought the town's beloved Reverend Charles had killed Tanya.

No, he was better off trying to put the past behind him. There were some things a man couldn't change, some things not worth the effort. Maybe a few weeks spent as Anna Rose's handyman would serve as a stopgap between his past and his uncertain future. A few weeks of blessed anonymity. Days spent working to the point of exhaustion, seeing no one except Anna Rose—a woman whose laughter reminded him that there was still some good left in the world.

Three

———

Anna Rose placed her beige heels in the shoe rack, then hung up her suit in the closet before stripping out of her slip and panty hose. Rummaging around in the bottom drawer of the oak chest, she found her blue bathing suit. It was a modest-cut one-piece she'd had for years. It did nothing to enhance her large-boned physique, but its simple lines weren't unflattering to her generously proportioned body.

All during church, much to her shame, she'd thought of nothing except Britt Cameron. He'd been her replacement handyman for a week and, with each passing day, she liked him more and more. As she peeled off her bra and panties, she wondered if *like* was too mild a word for the emotion Britt had stirred to life within her. She pulled on her bathing suit, reached into her closet for a wraparound cotton skirt, put it on and tied the string belt.

While she had sung hymns this morning, she'd been planning a picnic lunch with Britt down by the pond. And all the while Brother Sherman had admonished the congregation to be on guard against sin, she had been thinking about the past week, all the breakfasts and lunches she had shared with her new employee.

She had another ten days to go before her summer vacation officially began, but for her students, school had ended last Friday. The final days were always hectic, especially for the principal, but she'd made time to prepare breakfast every morning. Britt had been punctual, knocking on her door at six-thirty. And she had taken special pleasure in fixing a large, hardy supper every night. Although their evening meal usually lasted nearly two hours and they enjoyed each other's company, as soon as he'd helped her with the dishes, Britt always left. They discussed her job, the farm and how their individual days had gone, but he seemed reluctant to talk about himself or his life before the night he'd wrecked his truck in front of her house. Occasionally he'd mention his mother, brother or sisters. From bits and pieces of conversation, she'd learned his brother was married and had children.

She had longed to explain her problem to him, to ask if he would be willing to share in the solution, but finding herself growing more and more attracted to him each day made it difficult for her to ask him to pose as her fiancé. She didn't know what to make of Britt Cameron and the way he made her feel. Not once had he been anything but a perfect gentleman. He never touched her, never intimated that he was the least interested in her as a woman, and yet Anna Rose found herself daydreaming about him, fantasizing about what it would be like to kiss him, to be in his arms.

What would it take for her to finally learn? she asked herself. Men weren't attracted to her. She was big and tall and plain. Men liked smaller women. Of course, she was smaller, a lot smaller, than Britt. Her keen intellect often intimidated men and her aggressive, take-charge attitude scared them away. But Britt Cameron, though not formally educated, seemed highly intelligent, and he acted more amused than offended by her bossiness.

Don't do this to yourself, she chided. *Enjoy Britt's company, work up enough courage to ask him to pose as your fiancé, but don't be stupid enough to imagine you're falling in love with him. You would have had a better chance of snagging Kyle Ross than you'll ever have of enticing a man like Britt Cameron. An inexperienced virgin like you wouldn't have a prayer of attracting a man as virile as Britt.*

During the time it took her to prepare a huge picnic lunch and pack it, Anna Rose had convinced herself that what she felt for Britt was a growing friendship. And as she walked over to the sharecropper's shack, she told herself that hiring him had been a stroke of genius on her part. Not only did he work tirelessly all day, he provided companionship at meals, and might, if she could work up the courage to proposition him, solve her *mystery* fiancé problem.

The sun was at its afternoon high, radiating warmth and light over everything within sight. Overhead a clear blue sky spread from horizon to horizon like an enormous azure canopy, and a gentle spring wind rippled through the trees, so light as to be almost indiscernible. The day was so perfect it defied description, Anna Rose thought as she made her way along the path from her home to the old shack. With heavy picnic basket in one hand and folded towels and quilt in the other, she felt God's presence as much here in her woods, on this piece of earth that she had inherited from generations of Palmers, as she had today sitting in church.

She stopped short when she saw Britt sitting on the porch, his back propped up against the house. Anna Rose swallowed, heat rising within her as she gazed at his big, hairy body clad only in a pair of cutoff jeans. He seemed to be relaxing and totally unaware of her presence. She knew she should say something to him, but all she could do was stare.

What was it about this man that stirred such primitive emotions within her? she wondered. No man, not even the handsome and charming Kyle Ross, had ever created such chaos in her mind and heart. And in her body. Every time she looked at Britt, she felt ashamed of her body's traitorous reaction. She had never been with a man, but she wasn't so ignorant of human nature that she didn't recognize desire, especially when she was consumed by it.

Tarnation. Double, triple tarnation. She didn't need this, certainly didn't want this complication in her life. Maybe she should just turn around and go back home.

Too late. He'd spotted her, was looking directly at her.

"Hey there." He stood up slowly, then took a step in her direction, stopping just as his bare feet touched the first wooden step. "Sorry about the way I'm dressed. I wasn't expecting company."

"Don't apologize." She tried to smile, but the effort proved useless. She was too caught up in her own emotions to sympathize with his apparent embarrassment at her finding him partially undressed. "I—I thought we might go over to the pond and have a picnic for lunch today."

"I, er, was going to change into jeans and a shirt before coming up to the house for lunch. You said two o'clock." He turned around, took several steps, then grasped the handle on the screen door.

"Change of plans," she said, praying her voice didn't give away her nervousness. "Since it's such a beautiful day, I thought... Well, there's no need for you to change...unless you have swim trunks."

"Nope." He released the door handle, turned halfway around, and gave her a tentative smile. "Are you sure it's all right? I could at least put on a shirt."

"No need, unless you're worried about sunburn."

He glanced down at his darkly tanned torso and shook his head.

"Forget it," she said, feeling more a fool with each passing minute. Of course he wasn't worried about sunburn. His naturally dark complexion had taken on an almost bronze hue in the week he'd been working for her. She knew he went without a shirt some days. But never once had he come to her house without one. "Let's go. I'm starving." She tried for a light, friendly tone, knowing that if Britt even suspected she wanted him, he'd run as far and fast as he could.

"Just let me put this up," he said, reaching down to where he'd been sitting to pick up an open paperback book lying on the porch. "I've enjoyed reading the other two, and started this one about an hour ago."

She saw that he held one of the Dick Francis novels she'd loaned him earlier in the week. She had seen him looking at her huge collection of books and had asked if he enjoyed reading. He'd eyed her most recent purchase, a romance novel, lying on her desk, and told her his taste in reading material didn't run to romance or to poetry. That was when she'd gone to the shelf and retrieved three of her favorite Dick Francis mysteries, and was surprised that Britt was familiar with the author.

When he came back out of the house, he was wearing an unbuttoned, short-sleeved shirt. Neither of them mentioned his apparel. He took the heavy picnic basket and load of towels, leaving her to carry only the quilt.

"Lead the way," he said, following.

"An underground spring feeds the pond, you know," she told him as they walked along the narrow path that meandered through the woods.

"There's one on our property at home like that. We used to swim in it all the time when we were kids. Ma always made sure there were at least two of us together. She didn't take chances with our safety."

"I used to slip out here and just sit by the pond. My grandmother was very strict. She never allowed me to own a bathing suit, but Gramps taught me how to swim, anyway. I just wore loose pants." Anna Rose didn't like to remember the unpleasant things about her childhood, the horrible lectures Grandma had given her about the evils that lurked everywhere. Indeed Grandma had thought that anything that gave a person too much pleasure had to be a sin.

"Overly religious, huh?" Britt asked. "I had an aunt like that. My father's aunt, actually. Ma despised Aunt Methel.

Said she committed more sins in her fanaticism than most folks did just living life the best they knew how."

"Here we are," she said, thankful that they had arrived at the pond. She never discussed the details of her restricted upbringing with anyone, and doing so with Britt made her feel uncomfortable. Even she and Gramps had never really talked about the situation. Her grandfather had just accepted his wife as if he had no other choice, telling Anna Rose that her grandmother meant well. She had never understood what the outgoing, fun-loving David Palmer had had in common with his taciturn, sour-faced wife.

"This is nice," Britt said, glancing around at the tree-shaded pond, appreciating the peacefulness and solitude. "It's a lot like our pond."

"In Mississippi?" she asked as she spread the quilt on the ground.

"Yeah, in Mississippi." It was the first time she'd asked him about where he'd come from, and he didn't think, even now, she was being nosy. "I grew up on a farm in Riverton. My mother still lives there with my brother and his family. My sisters moved away as soon as they finished high school, but they visit from time to time."

"Riverton?" Anna Rose had been to Riverton, or rather, had ridden through Riverton on her way to Memphis. But that had been years ago, before the four-lane highway came through and bypassed all the small towns between Cherokee, Alabama and Corinth, Mississippi.

"You've been there?"

"Through there. Years ago. It's in Tishomingo County, isn't it?"

Britt stacked the towels at the edge of the quilt and set the basket in the center. "Yeah. Do you want me help you unpack?"

"No, no. Just sit down. I'll fix everything. Are you hungry?"

"Starving." He sat, stretching his long legs out in front of him. "Did your grandmother teach you how to cook?"

"Yes, as a matter of fact she did." Anna Rose sat down and began lifting out parcels covered in aluminum foil and clear plastic wrap. "Grandma was an excellent cook, and she thought every woman should know how. She considered it a duty."

"But you like to do it, don't you? It's a pleasure for you."

Amazing, she thought, that he understood. She did indeed like to cook, loved to, as a matter of fact. "It's been fun having someone to cook for besides myself," she said, then stole a glance at him to see if he might have misinterpreted her admission.

"Believe me, the pleasure has been mine."

He watched while she prepared them both a plate. By the time she poured the iced tea into tall, blue plastic cups, he was drooling. Fried chicken, potato salad, deviled eggs, baked beans and big, fluffy yeast rolls covered the large paper plate she handed him. When he took the plate, she delved into the basket and brought out blue paper napkins, along with plastic forks and spoons.

"What a feast," he said, setting the plate in his lap and situating the cup between his knees. Eyeing the napkin she laid at his side, he nodded his thanks. "You must like blue."

"You noticed."

"Yeah. A blue kitchen. A blue bathroom. Touches of blue in your living room. And you even wear a lot of blue."

"It's my favorite color." She glanced down at the blue bathing suit she wore and the blue flowered skirt that covered her from waist to mid-calf.

Britt's gaze followed hers, hesitating at the top edge of her bathing suit where her breasts swelled invitingly, then his gaze traveled the long length of her body and finally stopped at her feet, clad in a pair of slip-on white sandals. Unwillingly his thoughts filled with images of Anna Rose the way she had looked in her thin cotton nightgown the morning after he'd spent the night on her couch. What would she look like naked? he wondered. Would the rest of her body be as pale and smooth as her arms and legs, her long neck and broad shoulders?

"Let's eat," he said, his voice a harsh grumble.

She eyed him with a questioning glare. "Is something wrong?"

"No. I'm just hungry." The last thing he needed was to become embroiled in a relationship with Anna Rose. She wasn't the type of woman with whom a man could share a brief, meaningless affair. And God knew, he never again wanted to try to have a lasting relationship with a woman.

They ate in silence for endless minutes, neither looking up from their plates. Suddenly Lord Byron came bounding through the woods, rushing headlong into the middle of their picnic. Both Britt and Anna Rose held tightly to their plates, but the big rottweiler slammed into Anna Rose's side, knocking her tea out of her hand. The cool liquid spread quickly into the quilt and over Anna Rose's skirt.

"Oh, Lord Byron, you big baby. Where have you been?" she asked. "Out courting Murphy?" She glanced over at Britt, who held his plate in one hand and a drumstick in the other. "Murphy is my nearest neighbor's Labrador retriever."

"Is Lord Byron a ladies' man?"

"I'm afraid he's a regular Don Juan." Anna Rose laid her plate on the quilt, put two pieces of chicken on another plate and placed it at the edge of the quilt. Lord Byron, knowing from experience that the dish had been set aside for him, stretched out in the grass and began devouring his meager feast. "He's also a glutton. I can't fill him up. He not only looks like a small horse, he eats like one, too."

"We had a couple of German Shepherds when we were kids. Lily was only about three and she'd ride Wolf around like he was a pony."

"Lily is your baby sister, right?"

"Yeah. Wade's the oldest. He's thirty-four. Then me, two years younger, then Amy, three years younger than me, and finally Lily, who's just turned twenty-six."

"Are either of your sisters married?" Anna Rose nibbled on a roll.

"Not now. Amy married right after high school and left home. The marriage only lasted a couple of years." Britt didn't like to think about what bad luck the Cameron bunch had had in their marriages. The eldest three had all been divorced. Of course, Wade was happily married now. "Lily's still single."

"It must be wonderful to have brothers and sisters."

"You were an only child?"

"Yes."

"You told me that you were raised by your grandparents, that your grandmother was very religious and very strict, but you've never mentioned your parents."

"I never knew my father. He and my mother were just kids when she got pregnant. His parents sent him off to college and my sixteen-year-old mother gave birth to an illegitimate child and shamed her parents. I don't think my grandmother ever forgave my mother or...or me."

"Anna Rose..."

"It's all right. There's no more pain. I put it aside years ago. I've never even met my father. He and his family moved to California when he was still in college."

"Your mother—"

"Committed suicide when I was ten months old."

He laid his plate and cup aside, reached out and pulled her toward him. She hesitated momentarily, uncertain and afraid. Knowing that he intended to comfort her, Anna Rose wasn't sure she could go into his arms and not want more than sympathy.

"Please don't feel sorry for me," she said.

"Oh, Annie Rosie." He pulled her closer as he leaned over to take her in his arms, cradling her head in the curve of his shoulder. "Did your grandmother teach you to hide your feelings?"

"Grandma was Grandma. Gramps kept me sane, made me feel as if I were worthy of being alive." She couldn't bear to think about all the times her grandmother had ridiculed her, had scolded and punished her for crimes so infinitesimal that other parents would have dismissed them without a thought. Everything had been a sin. Parties. School dances. Dating. Kissing. Bathing suits. Shorts. Movies. Grandma had taken away every possible pleasure from her life, except her books. Anna Rose had kept them hidden in her room.

"When did she die?" he asked, wondering how many years Anna Rose had been forced to endure the old woman's mental cruelties.

"When I was eighteen and away at college. I had graduated from high school at sixteen and earned a full scholarship to the University of Alabama. When Grandma died, I came home and went to U.N.A. so I could be here to help Gramps."

"A full scholarship at sixteen?" She'd told him she was an elementary school principal, so he'd assumed she was college educated. He knew she was very intelligent, but suspected her intellect had often been more of a curse than a blessing. "What's your IQ, Annie Rosie? Are you a genius?"

She flushed, embarrassed instead of proud. Well-meaning friends and relatives had told her often enough that most men didn't like women who were smarter than they. Her cousin Tammy had cautioned her when she'd been dating Kyle Ross. But he hadn't seemed to object to the fact that she was intelligent, and it hadn't seemed to bother him that she was the principal and he a teacher. But then, he had never been seriously interested in her. They'd dated numerous times, and she had allowed her infatuation to cloud her vision, had seen love when only friendship had existed.

"No, I'm not a genius," she said, relaxing against Britt when he began to run his hand up and down her back in a soothing gesture. "But I am intelligent."

"And a good cook."

"What?" She raised her head from his shoulder.

"I said not only are you intelligent, but you're a good cook." He knew he'd said the right thing when she smiled, then started laughing.

Her laughter warmed his cold heart, the sound sweet to his ears. He refused to examine too closely the reasons why it was important to him to see her smile, to ease her pain and try to erase the bad memories.

"You're good for me, Britt Cameron," she said, looking him squarely in the eye. Her breath caught in her throat at the intense way he was staring at her. It was as if he could see straight through to her soul. Confused and a little frightened, she pulled away from him. "Why don't we go for a swim?"

"So soon after eating? I'm afraid I'd sink to the bottom of the pond." He tried to make the tone of his voice light and teasing. He'd seen that look of confusion in her eyes, had felt her hesitation. Had she realized that, for one split second, the thought of making love to her had crossed his mind? Hell, he didn't want to make love to Anna Rose. She wasn't his type. Besides, she was becoming his friend, and he'd never had a female friend before. He didn't want to louse up the easy companionship they shared when all he needed was a quick tumble. Any woman would do for that. Any woman except Anna Rose.

"Well, you sit here and let your lunch settle." She patted him on his flat stomach, then jerked her hand away. "I'm going for a swim."

He watched her jump up, discarding her skirt before running to the pond. She dived in, swimming with swift even strokes. Her touch had been innocent, a teasing gesture, but he could still feel the imprint of her long fingers, their warmth spreading through him like a slowly growing flame. She'd felt it, too. That was why she'd jerked her hand away.

Something was wrong, damned wrong when a woman like Anna Rose could arouse him. Hell, what he needed was a couple of nights in some sexy little blonde's bed.

Anna Rose simply wasn't the kind of woman a man fantasized about. But she sure was the type to comfort a man, to give his heart and mind ease. She seemed to know instinctively when he needed to be alone and exactly when he needed her company. For eight days he'd shared meals with her as well as good conversation and genuine companionship. She never pried, but he knew she'd listen if he wanted to talk. The funny thing was that all during the day when he was working, he'd think about her. At odd times, something she'd said would pop into his mind—the way she blushed when she was embarrassed—the sound of her laughter.

He stood up and walked over to lean against an enormous maple tree. Folding his arms across his chest, he stared out at the pond, his gaze riveted to Anna Rose. She had stopped swimming and stood near the water's edge, her body visible from the knees up. She'd turned her face toward the sun, allowing her long hair to fall in a wet, tangled mass down her back. For such a large woman, she wasn't built half bad, he thought. A couple of generations ago, her generous proportions would have been considered perfect.

The sunlight glistened off the moisture coating her skin and it turned her hair to a silvery tan. Drops of water clung to her face. For one split second, Britt looked at her and thought she was lovely.

As if drawn by a force he was powerless to resist, Britt flung his unbuttoned shirt on the ground, ran up behind Anna Rose and grabbed her around the waist, flinging them both into the pond. They went under, then resurfaced quickly.

Wiping the water from her eyes as she coughed several times, Anna Rose faced him. "What were you trying to do, drown me?" she asked, unable to mask her smile.

"Why didn't you tell me the water was this cold?" Giving a mock shudder, he ran his hands up and down his arms, as if trying to warm himself.

"It's not cold, just cool." She scooped up water in both hands and flung it at him, laughing when he spluttered.

"You're going to be sorry for that, Annie Rosie." When he reached out for her, she swam away toward the opposite side of the pond.

He followed suit, catching up with her just as she made a mad scramble onto dry ground. He swung her up in his arms, spinning her around and around before tossing her back into the pond. She hit the water with a resounding splash. Standing on the bank, he broke into peals of laughter. While watching her swim back to the other side, the thought struck him that only a week ago he'd been sure he'd never laugh again. Tanya's betrayal, her subsequent death and then the nightmare trial had taken all the laughter from his life—what little there had been since Paul's death almost five years ago.

Britt walked around the edge of the pond, making his way back to the quilt where Anna Rose sat, drying herself off with a huge blue-and-white striped towel.

"We never did eat dessert," he said, slumping down beside her as he reached for a towel.

"You're a bottomless pit."

His gaze settled on her mouth, still damp from her swim. A single drop of water fell from her lips onto her chin. The sunlight caught on that one transparent particle, creating a tiny pastel rainbow inside. Britt had the strangest urge to lick away that magic touch of moisture.

While he dried off, she brought out a bundle of fried pies, placing one on a napkin. "Here. I made fried peach pies."

Tossing his damp towel aside, he accepted the treat, immediately taking a huge bite. After swallowing, he said, "I can't believe some man hasn't married you just for your cooking." The moment he looked at her face, he regretted his choice of words. Her stunned expression was enough to make him wish he'd bitten his tongue. "Ah, you're probably one of those career women who doesn't want to be tied down to a man. I mean considering your education and career.''

Well, it's time to tell him, she decided. *He's given you the perfect opening to ask him the big question.* ''I'd like to get married and have children, but I seem to scare men.''

''Look, you don't have to—''

''Last fall I made a complete fool of myself over a new male teacher. His name is Kyle Ross, and I misunderstood the friendly attention he paid me. We dated several times, and I thought I was in love. Everyone in Cherokee thought that, finally, poor Anna Rose had found herself a man.'' Once started, she couldn't stop talking, but when he grabbed her by the shoulders, she ceased her incessant babbling. ''What?''

He didn't like to see her this way, baring her soul. He could actually feel her pain. ''There's no need for you to tell me about this.''

''Yes, there is.'' With more courage than she knew she possessed, she looked him squarely in the eye. ''I need your help.''

''What sort of help?''

''Let me explain.'' She swallowed hard and took a deep breath before continuing. ''Kyle didn't really lead me on. He didn't need to, I was so infatuated with him. But he never once told me that there was someone else. Just when I and the whole town thought he was ready to pop the question, he married his college sweetheart. He just went home for Spring Break in March and came back married.''

''My God. What a bastard.'' Britt thought that if he could get hold of this Kyle Ross, he'd give him a much needed lesson in the right way to treat a woman like Anna Rose.

''Not really. I simply read more into our relationship than was there.'' *The same way I'm doing now—with you,* she reminded herself. Only the way she had felt about Kyle was nothing compared to her feelings for Britt. She had never wanted Kyle, not in that basic, sexually hungry way she wanted Britt. She'd never been with a man, but every time she got near Britt, she started thinking about what it would be like if he made love to her.

"Did he kiss you?" Britt asked, releasing his tight hold on her arms. "Embrace you? Whisper sweet nothings in your ear?"

"Ah, er, yes." Kyle had been smooth, a practiced ladies' man. He'd had every female teacher at Cherokee Elementary swooning over him.

"Did he ever...?" Britt wanted to ask her if she'd ever allowed Kyle Ross to make love to her, hating the very thought of another man touching her. Not that he cared, personally, he told himself. It's just that he'd hate to think the guy had seduced her. "Just how serious was your relationship?"

"He did ask me to sleep with him, if that's what you're asking." Anna Rose remembered how tempted she'd been to have sex with Kyle, not because she'd wanted him so desperately, but because she longed to know what it was all about, longed to lose her virginity and become a real woman.

Suddenly Britt felt like smashing his fist into something, and wished Kyle Ross's face was handy. "Damn him."

"I didn't," she said, her voice delicately soft and filled with vulnerability.

"You didn't have sex with him?"

"No. I considered it, but while I was trying to make up my mind, he married someone else."

"You're better off without him."

"I've come to that conclusion on my own, but I still have a problem to deal with." She braced herself, hoping her courage wouldn't fail her now.

"What problem?"

"After Kyle's unexpected marriage, all my friends and relatives... well, practically the whole town felt sorry for me." She almost let her gaze falter when she saw a glimmer of sympathy in his eyes. "People have felt sorry for me my whole life. Poor Anna Rose, born out of wedlock. Poor

Anna Rose's mother killed herself. Poor Anna Rose who took care of her elderly grandparents. Poor Anna Rose, with her plain looks and bossy personality, she'll never get a man.''

''People can be cruel,'' he said, thinking of himself as much as her. She couldn't bear her townspeople's pity; he couldn't bear his townspeople's distrust.

''I did a stupid thing. I told my friend Edith that everyone had been mistaken about my feelings for Kyle...that all the while he'd had a secret lover, so had I.''

''What?''

''I told Edith that I had met a man on my vacation last summer and we'd been corresponding ever since, and...well...that he'd asked me to marry him and I'd accepted.''

''But there is no man, no fiancé?'' he asked, knowing full well that she'd concocted the lie to protect herself.

''That was a couple of months ago, and people are asking when my mystery fiancé is going to show up.'' She wanted to ask him to pose as that fiancé, but somehow she couldn't make the words form on her lips.

''You have boxed yourself into a corner, haven't you?''

''If I don't come up with a fiancé, and soon, I'm going to wind up looking like more of a fool than I would have if I'd just gone ahead and let everyone feel sorry for me.'' *Please, Britt, don't you realize that you're the solution to my problem?*

He understood her predicament and realized that she was trying to ask him to pose as her fiancé. Without even thinking, he said, ''Would it help if you passed me off as your mystery man?''

The smile that spread across her face overrode the shock he felt by his own words. He hadn't meant to volunteer, but he had allowed his emotions to overrule his common sense. It was a habit he needed to break, one for which he'd already paid dearly.

''Would you? Oh, Britt, would you really?''

"I don't want to be paraded around, go to parties or church or whatever, but I'm sure if I stay another few weeks, sooner or later someone is going to notice I'm here. When they do, just say I'm your fiancé." What the hell, he thought, what harm would it do to help out a nice lady like Anna Rose? It seemed to him she'd had too many tough breaks in her life. Even if he couldn't make his own life any easier, maybe he could hers.

"No, no, you won't have to do anything," she assured him. "When you leave, I'll simply say that we had a serious quarrel and I asked you to go...that I decided you were the wrong man for me."

"Okay. Sounds like something we can both handle."

"Then you will? You'll pretend to be my fiancé for a few weeks?"

"Sure, why not?"

Not expecting what happened next, Britt was caught totally off guard when she threw her arms around him and kissed him soundly on the mouth. As if sensing that she'd made a serious faux pas, Anna Rose jerked away from him. "Oh, Britt, I'm sorry. I didn't mean to do that. Really. It's just that I'm so grateful. Tarnation, Britt, say something."

Instead of saying anything, he reacted on a purely instinctive level. Pulling her into his arms, he gave her a quick, hard kiss. "That's to seal our bargain."

"Oh." Her lips formed a soft, moist oval.

Kissing her had been a mistake. She'd been so warm and compliant. He hadn't kissed a woman in a long time, too long a time, he thought as he again covered her mouth with his. Damn, she was sweet. Her lips parted, eagerly accepting the thrust of his tongue as he deepened the kiss, turning it from a gentle invasion into a thorough ravaging. She moaned when his arms encircled her, hauling her up against him, crushing her breasts into his chest.

Anna Rose had never been kissed so completely in all her life. She felt as if her bones were dissolving, that if Britt didn't hold on to her, she would melt away. As abruptly as he'd taken her mouth, he released it.

"Hey, hey, Annie Rosie, we're unofficially, officially engaged." He couldn't—wouldn't—allow himself to use this woman, he thought, looking at her, seeing the passion so evident in her eyes. He was aroused. She was needy. What he felt was lust, but a woman like Anna Rose would call it love. No way in hell was he going to hurt her. She'd been hurt enough. He could never love her, so he had no right to take from her when he had nothing to give in return.

"Thanks, Britt," she said, glancing down at her long, full thighs, hating herself for not being little and slim and desirable.

Jumping up, he grabbed both of her hands and helped her to her feet. "Come on, let's take another swim before heading back."

Without giving her time to reply, he scooped her up in his arms and ran into the cool water, not releasing her until they were in the middle of the pond. Slowly, ever so slowly, he eased her down his body. She gasped when she felt his arousal.

She swam away from him before he could see the tears in her eyes. He was aroused and yet he didn't want her, she thought. *Am I so undesirable? He needs a woman and yet he'd rather do without than to make love to me.*

Anna Rose knew now that she'd never been in love before, most definitely not with Kyle Ross. But she suspected that she was falling in love with Britt and realized there was little hope of his ever returning her affections.

Knowing that, she dreaded the next few weeks. She would see him every day and would eventually be introducing him as her fiancé. How was she going to be able to live a lie when, with every beat of her heart, she'd be wishing it was true?

Four

The setting sun's warmth was spread by the wind's gentle breath as it floated through the trees and grass and flowers. The fragrance of honeysuckle wafted in the breeze, combining with the smell of freshly plowed earth and the refreshing, natural aroma of country air. Britt loved the land, and couldn't imagine living in the city. The never-ending noise, the constant commotion, the filth of so many people crammed together in a small area, not to mention the odor, the smog and the high crime rate. No, some people might enjoy a more hectic life-style, might actually prefer the hustle and bustle associated with city living, but not Britt Cameron. His sisters seemed happy enough living away from the farm, but he knew he would never be content anywhere but in the country. Four years in the marines had proven that fact to him years ago.

Britt checked his watch. He'd taken time to shower and change clothes as he did every evening before walking from the sharecropper's shack over to Anna Rose's house for supper. After their picnic by the pond four days ago, they had both been careful not to allow their emotions to overrule their common sense. The next morning at breakfast, Britt had felt her uncertainty, her uncharacteristic shyness, and he'd tried to act as if nothing of any importance had transpired between them. Hell, all they'd done was kiss, he told himself. That *wasn't* anything important. At least it wouldn't have been to most women. But Anna Rose wasn't most women. The longer Britt knew her, the more he understood what an insecure and inexperienced woman she was. He suspected that she didn't know a damn thing about men.

He wasn't sure why, but concentrating on Anna Rose's problems seemed to divert his attention from his own. But that only made him feel all the more guilty for not telling her the complete truth about himself. If she was going to pass him off as her fiancé, she had a right to know that he'd been accused of his wife's murder, that half his hometown still thought he was guilty.

He didn't want Anna Rose to know that Tanya had been murdered, and that he'd gone to trial and only the lack of hard evidence freed him from a prison sentence. He didn't want to take the risk that she would turn from him and ask him to leave before he was ready to go. He'd found the first real peace he'd known in years here in Alabama, living in a shack, working as a handyman and sharing meals with a woman who looked at him with adoration in her eyes. He couldn't bear the thought of seeing that adoration turn to suspicion.

He liked Anna Rose. She was genuine and honest and didn't know the first thing about using feminine wiles to trap a man into making a fool of himself. She was the type of person who made a good friend, a congenial companion whose intelligent conversation was never boring. What surprised him the most about his relationship with Anna Rose was that, despite the fact she wasn't the type of woman who usually attracted him, he wanted her. And if she wasn't so damned inexperienced, he would pursue an affair with her. They were both lonely people dealing with a past neither of them could change. He had no doubts that they'd be as good for each other as lovers as they were as friends. The only problem was that when his temporary job ended, he'd have no problem saying goodbye and going on his way. But Anna Rose was the kind of woman who'd have sex and love all mixed up. She probably thought she couldn't have one without the other. He wouldn't risk letting her fall in love with him when he had no love left to give anyone.

Deep in thought, Britt emerged from the path onto Anna Rose's driveway, not noticing the big white Cadillac parked behind Anna Rose's Blazer. The petite blonde wearing skin-tight jeans and a hot-pink halter top caught his attention. She was stepping onto the porch, her small hips swaying seductively.

Damn, who is she? he wondered. Anna Rose hadn't mentioned expecting any company. Hoping he could make his way back along the path before the woman noticed him, Britt started to turn. Too late. She'd seen him.

"Hi, there." Her voice held a high-pitched, childlike quality.

Gritting his teeth and muttering imprecations, Britt stopped dead still. He didn't want to have to face this stranger, whoever she was, but it looked as if he had no choice. She was walking straight toward him.

Britt guessed she was in her late twenties. She was very attractive in a rather gaudy way. Her figure was good, but she wasn't really pretty. Perhaps that was the reason she wore too much makeup. Her pale blond hair was cut short. A pair of half-dollar-size gold hoops hung in her ears, three strands of gold chains draped her neck, a pair of gold bracelets circled each wrist and every finger was adorned with a ring.

"I'm Tammy Spires," she said, as if her name should mean something to him.

"Britt Cameron, ma'am." He could smell her perfume. Something heavy and spicy and liberally applied.

"My, oh, my, you must be Anna Rose's mystery man. I've just been dying to meet you." She giggled like a junior high cheerleader making a pass at a senior quarterback. "As a matter of fact, half the town's been wanting to get a glimpse of you. Edith Hendricks said she'd driven by five times hoping you'd be outside in the yard."

Tammy laid her hand on his arm, her long, hot-pink nails scraping his skin. He looked down into her big blue eyes. Smiling, she giggled again, and he thought of Tanya. This woman reminded him of his dead wife. She was about the same size, had the same coloring, the same childish laugh and the same coquettish way of flirting with a man. Just as he started to move away from Tammy, he heard the front door open and looked across the yard. Anna Rose walked out onto the front porch.

"I see you've met Britt," Anna Rose said.

"Your fiancé." Tammy sighed. "Who would ever have believed it." Tightening her hold on Britt, she laced her nails through the curly hair on his forearm. "I must say, he isn't quite what I expected."

Not caring if he appeared rude, Britt pulled away from the blonde's tenacious grasp. When he did, she gave him an amused look, then walked away. Britt watched her join Anna Rose on the porch, wishing he could escape, but knowing Anna Rose was counting on his cooperation. He'd promised that he'd pose as her fiancé, and he was a man of his word.

Anna Rose hated the old feelings of jealousy she'd always secretly harbored against her cousin Tammy, and had thought she'd long since overcome such a fruitless emotion. But seeing Tammy practically drooling all over Britt had given new life to the old green-eyed monster within her.

"How nice to see you, Tammy," Anna Rose said, forcing a smile. "What brings you out this way?"

"Nothing special. Just thought I'd drop by and see how you're doing. Of course, word's all over Cherokee that you've got a man staying in the old shack over in the woods."

"Britt, come on in. Supper's almost ready." Anna Rose opened the front door, looking over Tammy's shoulder to where Britt stood, silent and unmoving.

"Yeah," he finally said. "Sure thing."

Anna Rose didn't want to issue her cousin an invitation, but years of having hospitable Southern manners drilled into her superceded her own personal desire. "Won't you join us?"

Tammy couldn't seem to stop looking at Britt. Anna Rose didn't like the way she was sizing him up, as if she were measuring to see if he'd fit in her bed. "I'd love to stay, but I'm afraid Roy Dean's expecting me. We're driving up to Florence to eat at the Renaissance Tower."

Anna Rose watched while Britt walked slowly toward the house. She knew he wasn't pleased about Tammy's visit, about having to actually begin the pretense. "Well, come on in and stay a few minutes. I'll get us all some tea."

Anna Rose held the door open for Tammy to enter, then waited until Britt came up behind her before taking a step. Unexpectedly he put his arm around her waist and led her inside. His arm was big and warm and strong. She loved the feel of it about her, the gentle power in his embrace. She knew he was acting affectionate for Tammy's sake, but even a pretense of caring was more than Anna Rose had expected.

"Who is she?" he asked, his mouth at Anna Rose's ear.

"My cousin." Her reply came on a whispered sigh.

He nuzzled her neck. She trembled. "Loosen up," he said under his breath. "We're engaged. Remember?"

Tammy eyed Britt's arm about Anna Rose's waist, then flashed him her most seductive smile. "Now, tell me, just what on earth do you and our Anna Rose have in common?"

"Besides love?" he asked, deciding in that one moment that he didn't much care for Cousin Tammy. It was obvious the conceited little bitch didn't think Anna Rose could attract a man.

Tammy giggled again, but this time the sound had a false ring to it. "Yes, of course. Love, hmm?"

Standing in the middle of her living room, Anna Rose was thankful for Britt's arm about her, giving her support and encouragement. She had always felt so plain and plump and tall beside her colorful, petite cousin. "Well, Britt and I love the land since we both grew up on a farm. He grew up in Mississippi. We both appreciate the simple pleasures."

"Honey, why don't you sit down and have a visit with Tammy while I go fix us all some tea," Britt said, just before he kissed her on the cheek and gave her an affectionate squeeze.

Open-mouthed and wide-eyed, Anna Rose stared at Britt. He smiled at her. She released a breath she hadn't even realized she was holding and smiled back at him. "Thank you . . . sweetheart. That would be nice."

The minute Britt left the room, Tammy grabbed Anna Rose by the arm. "Honey? Sweetheart? My, my, how lovey-dovey y'all are."

"Sit down, Tammy." Anna Rose hadn't dreaded a visit from her cousin in years, but she did this evening.

"What's he like in bed?" Tammy asked, and laughed loudly when Anna Rose blushed. "Good God, how on earth do you think you can hold on to someone like that? There's a lot of man there, cousin. More than you can handle, I'd say."

Anna Rose closed her eyes for a brief second, praying for the patience to live through the next few minutes without giving Tammy a proper tongue-lashing. The two had locked horns before, years ago, and although Anna Rose could out-think and out-talk Tammy, her own insecurities always gave her cousin the upper hand.

Opening her eyes, Anna Rose smiled at Tammy. "You'd better not stay for tea. Roy Dean's probably waiting on you right now. Besides, supper is ready and I was looking forward to sharing a romantic meal with my fiancé."

"Getting all huffy, are we?" Tammy gave Anna Rose a long, critical appraisal. "What's the matter? Afraid Britt likes my looks better than yours? You ought to be used to that by now. I can't help being cute any more than you can help being plain."

Britt carried a tray of tall frosty glasses when he walked into the room. "Well, I'll admit that you're all right for a skinny little girl," he said, setting the tray down on the coffee table, then raising his eyes to meet Anna Rose's startled gaze. "But I prefer tall, bosomy women. I've never known a woman that I find more appealing than my Annie Rosie."

Later, Anna Rose decided that she would have given a year's pay to have had a camera handy and taken a snapshot of Tammy's face. Dazed. Shocked. Total disbelief. It was one of the absolutely best moments of Anna Rose's life.

Her cousin had muttered something about being late and having to leave, then she'd walked briskly out of the room. As if hoping to attract Britt's attention, she slowed to a leisurely saunter as she swayed her hips on the way to the front door.

"Thank you," Anna Rose said as she wiped the happy tears from her eyes, bursting into laughter as she fell backward onto the couch.

Laughing almost as hard, Britt slumped down beside her. God, how he loved the sound of Anna Rose's laughter.

Britt spooned the last bite of blackberry cobbler into his mouth, savoring the lush sweetness of the berries and the rich buttery taste of the delicious crust. Moaning as he rested his spoon in the empty bowl, he shoved his chair back as he looked across the table at Anna Rose, who was finishing off her own generous helping of dessert.

"You're the only woman I've ever known who is a better cook than Ma."

"Never, ever, tell your mother that," Anna Rose advised.

"Hey, I may not have a college degree, but I'm not stupid."

"Does it bother you, not having a college education?" she asked, wondering if the fact that she did would prove to be an obstacle to the romantic relationship she longed for them to share. Her education and a man's lack of one had proven to be a strike against her when it came to finding a husband.

"Hell, no." Britt picked up his glass of iced tea. "If I'd wanted to go to college I could have used the GI bill when I got out of the marines." He swallowed the remainder of his tea, then set the glass back on the table. "I'm a country boy, with farming in my blood, rich black earth under my fingernails and manure on my boots."

Anna Rose smiled at his self-analysis. "Well, I'm just as much of a country girl as you are a country boy. But I never did excel at being a girl or a woman, so I realized that being a farmer's wife with a passel of kids running around probably wasn't in my future."

"Did you ever try?" he asked, running his big hand up and down the moist tea glass.

"Ever try what?"

"To excel at being a woman?" The thought that someone, probably her grandmother, had stunted Anna Rose's natural feminine growth made him wish that he could do something to help her reach her full potential as a woman.

She felt the flush begin at the back of her neck and knew her cheeks were turning pink. "I'm sure you noticed that Tammy excels at being a woman. I found that out when we were teenagers."

"Tammy excels at flaunting herself," Britt said, tightening his hold on the glass, angered at Anna Rose's lack of self-esteem. Didn't she realize that she was twice the woman her cousin was? "You're not the type, honey. You wouldn't even begin to know how to seduce a man, would you?"

"No." Tarnation. Double, triple tarnation! What was the matter with her? Here she was admitting to Britt, the man she was falling in love with, what a failure she was as a woman. And he was feeling sorry for her.

"Your grandmother really did a number on you, didn't she?" When he heard her gasp and saw the stricken look on her face, he almost regretted his rash question. Almost. If Anna Rose had never dealt with the emotional abuse he suspected she'd suffered as a child, then she would never be free from the past. He'd learned that the hard way. He had never allowed himself to come to terms with Paul's death, with his own guilt over the accident, so he'd married Paul's widow as some blind act of contrition.

"Grandmother was very moral. Nothing was more important to her that what other people thought of her, how they perceived her, and . . . and what sort of impression her family made. I don't think she ever completely recovered from my mother's unwed pregnancy and subsequent suicide."

"Did she blame herself?" He watched the subtle change in Anna Rose's blue eyes, a hint of moisture glazing the surface, a delicate narrowing as if preparing to close and blot out the truth.

"No. She blamed me." Anna Rose's breath came in quick, jerky gulps. Clutching the edge of the dining-room table with her fingers, she tried to control her erratic heartbeat.

Britt scooted his chair farther from the table and stood, never once removing his gaze from Anna Rose. Had he pushed her too far with such a blunt question? Facing the truth wasn't easy, and he suspected this was the first time she'd ever said the words aloud. "It's all right, honey. Don't hold back." He rounded the table in a swift but smooth move.

When he knelt down, squatting beside her chair, she looked at him, large crystal drops of moisture caught in the corners of her eyes. "Everything was always my fault." She gulped down the first onslaught of tears. "I was always doing something wrong. I was too noisy, too messy, too tall, too big, too plain." She felt his hands lifting hers, encompassing them within his gentle grasp.

"Go on. What else?" He encouraged her to release all the repressed anger and pain within her. He knew what guilt felt like, no matter how senseless. He'd lived with it every day of his life since Paul's death.

"Gramps was a good man, but he wasn't strong enough to stand up to Grandmother. Maybe...maybe he was dealing with guilt of his own. I don't know." Anna Rose bit her bottom lip in a effort to keep from crying. The hurt inside her had spread from her heart into her chest and throat and stomach. Her emotional pain had become a physical ache. "Gramps was kindhearted, and so gentle. Too gentle to cope with Grandmother. He loved animals. We used to have horses. And he kept pigs and cattle...and...and there were always dogs and cats and..."

"You got your love of animals from your grandfather." Britt tried to summon up some sympathy for the old man whose life had probably been made a living hell by his wife, but all Britt could think about was how badly Anna Rose must have needed her gramps's support and care. Maybe he'd given her all he was capable of giving. God knew, no one could make another person feel something that wasn't in them to feel. He'd learned that lesson all too well with Tanya. He'd thought that if he loved her enough, she would eventually love him, too.

"When I started school, I found that I was smart, despite the fact that Grandmother often told me I wasn't as smart as my mother had been." She pulled her hands free from his, wiping the tears from her cheeks with her fingertips. "No matter what I did, how hard I tried, I could never please her. But she was proud of my accomplishments at school. I found that making good grades met with her approval."

"So you excelled at schoolwork—"

"I couldn't excel at anything else. I was big for my age, quite plain, and I found that, despite the fact that I hated it in her, I had inherited my grandmother's bossy personality. It drove the other kids crazy. I always acted like a mother or a big sister instead of a playmate."

"What happened when you got old enough to date?" He reached out and ran the forefinger of each hand under her damp eyes. He had become so accustomed to the way Anna Rose ignored his deformed hand that he didn't feel the least uncomfortable in caressing her with it.

"When was that?" she asked, laughing, the sound tight and dry and anguished.

"Didn't you date in high school?" He framed her face with his hands, and felt a sudden jolt of adrenaline shoot through his body. This face wasn't plain, he realized. It was a strong face. A face with character. Anna Rose would look the same forty years from now as she did today. Just a bit older with a few wrinkles, but her bone structure would do her proud in old age. Her eyes were the most incredible shade of blue—as pure as she. And her lips were so full and pouty and irresistible.

"No one ever asked me, except..."

"Except?" he asked.

"Howard Gene Dowdy."

"Did Howard Gene match his name?" Britt ran his hands down her neck and across her shoulders.

"Oh, yes." Anna Rose smiled, surprised that the memory wasn't so unpleasant anymore. "Pure redneck. He drove a truck with a Rebel flag on the back window. He was shorter and fatter than I was and so full of it you had to wear knee-high boots for protection."

"What happened with good ol' Howard Gene?" Taking her by the shoulders, Britt urged her to stand. "While you tell me about your first date, I'll help you clean up the dishes.''

She smiled, nodding agreement, then began helping him clear away the table. ''There was no first date. At least, not with Howard Gene Dowdy. Grandmother found out from Aunt Hattie that Tammy had engineered the date, had promised Howard Gene that if he'd take me to the senior prom, she'd go out on a date with him.''

''And your grandmother told you?'' Pushing open the kitchen door with his hip, he allowed her to enter first.

''Yes.'' She placed the dishes on the counter. ''Grandmother didn't approve of dancing, but hadn't forbidden me to attend the prom because she didn't think anyone would ask me. She knew telling me the truth about what Tammy had done was the easiest way to keep me from going.'' Anna Rose opened the dishwasher, stacking the dishes inside as she continued talking. ''Now, I wish I'd gone. I never attended a school dance. That was my only chance. And I was so angry with Tammy. I shouldn't have been. She meant well.''

Reaching down, Britt took her by the hands and pulled her up to face him. Holding her at arm's length, he smiled. ''Leave the dishes until later.''

''Why?'' She didn't hesitate to follow when, tugging on her hands, he led her out of the kitchen, down the hall and into the living room. He took her in his arms, spinning her around and around as if they were moving to some silent rhythm that only they could hear.

Twirling her back into his arms, Britt watched her face as it became vibrant with life, flushed with color, glowing with laughter. Her eyes sparkled with astonishment as she stared at him. ''What on earth are you doing?'' she asked, a hint of amused wonder in her question.

His gaze wandered over the room, lingering on the arrangement of fresh flowers that graced the mantel, their beauty reflected in the gold-framed mirror above the fireplace. With his hands at her waist, he pushed her backward. "Close your eyes, and stay right there while you think about being sixteen again. Picture yourself in a blue satin evening gown."

"What?" With amazed uncertainty she watched while he walked over to the stereo situated beneath the double windows. Opening the lid on her stash of cassettes, he flipped through them, then pulled out a tape and dropped it into the open slot.

Before moving from the stereo to the mantel, he turned, frowned at Anna Rose and shook his head. "I told you to close your eyes." He smiled when she obeyed.

He lifted a white rose from the flower arrangement. Since spending the past couple of weeks around Anna Rose, he'd found that she loved flowers and cut arrangements from her own flower beds to keep the house filled with springtime color, even on the darkest night or gloomiest day.

When he came near, she shivered. "Keep your eyes closed," he told her again, not stopping to ask himself why he was doing what he was doing.

Britt lifted the long tan strands of her hair away from her face, then slipped the thornless stem behind her ear, allowing the rose to lie nestled against her cheekbone.

"Britt?"

"What?" He took her in his arms just as the music began. The song was "Unchained Melody." Bill Medley's sensuous baritone voice filled every corner of the room.

"May I open my eyes now?" she asked as Britt moved his hand to rest slightly above her hip.

"Are you sixteen?"

"Am I...?" She suspected what he was trying to do, and loved him all the more for being so kind, but it broke her heart, just a little, to think that his motivation was pity. "Yes, I'm sixteen."

"Are you wearing a blue satin gown?"

She knew full well that she was wearing an old pair of loose-fitting blue slacks and a matching cotton sweater. "Yes, I'm wearing blue satin, and I'm ready for the prom."

She opened her eyes just in time to catch him watching her intently. In that one timeless moment, she knew she loved Britt Cameron. Loved his rough, scarred face. Loved his big, lean body. Loved his tender, caring heart.

"Good," he said, dancing with her to the hauntingly sweet tune that had enchanted more than one pair of lovers.

Without any words between them except the lyrics of the songs that played off the cassette tape, Britt danced with Anna Rose. Gradually their bodies drew closer and closer. She rested her head on his shoulder as she draped her arms around his neck. He lowered his left hand to her back while easing the right one down her hip.

When the music ended, their movements were already so languid that neither of them stopped. With her feet still shuffling as they followed his, Anna Rose raised her head and stared into his half-closed eyes.

"Why did you do this for me?"

It wasn't a question with an easy answer. The complete truth was a mystery to him. How could he explain that the weeks he'd spent as her handyman had saved his sanity, had given him solace when he'd thought he'd never find any, that he had felt more comfortable, more relaxed and at home here with her than he'd felt in years?

He couldn't remember the last time he'd met someone he liked as much as Anna Rose, and it seemed ages since he'd truly wanted to make love to a woman. But he couldn't—*wouldn't*—take advantage of Anna Rose's vulnerability. If he'd ever known a woman in need of loving, it was Anna Rose Palmer. But she deserved a man who'd be around for the long haul. A man capable of returning all the love she could give him. He wasn't that man.

"I'm sorry," she said, averting his intent stare. "I didn't realize the question would be so difficult for you to answer."

"You're a special lady, Annie Rosie. A lady who should have sweet memories of her senior prom." He lifted her downcast chin.

She refused to meet his gaze. "You feel sorry for me, don't you?"

He forced her chin higher, clutching her jaw in his forceful grasp. "I resent like hell what your grandmother did to you, what you keep doing to yourself, but I don't feel sorry for you."

Her eyes flew wide open. She glared at him. "Then why—"

"Look, you took in a stranger, gave him a job, a place to live. You took a risk allowing me to stay—"

"You're trying to repay me?" she asked.

"In a way." When she tried to pull away from him, he dropped his hand from her chin, but grabbed her by the waist. "Don't run away from me. Let me help you."

"Help me?" She stared at him, her eyes questioning as she struggled to free herself from his tenacious hold.

"I know I owe you a complete explanation, but...I... there are things about myself I'd rather not discuss. At least not tonight. Let's just say that having you trust me, care about me, share your life with me has meant more to me than you'll ever know."

"Oh, Britt."

He saw her eyes soften, her whole face brighten to what she considered a promise in his words. She relaxed against him, no longer struggling to escape. God, he couldn't let her misinterpret what he'd said. He couldn't let her think, not for one minute, that he could give her what she so desperately needed.

He released her. She swayed toward him, her eyes dreamy. "Look, honey, I realize that you don't know much about men."

"Is that a problem?" she asked.

"For you it is. You're the kind of woman who'd make some man a good wife, but, well—"

"What makes you think I want a husband?"

"Well, you do, don't you? Something tells me that you're the type of woman who needs a family."

"My career is very important. I love working with the children and their parents, with other teachers." She paused momentarily, surveying his face for a clue to where their conversation was headed. "You're right, I do want to marry and have a family."

"What you need are some lessons in how to excel at being a woman."

She felt a jolt of mixed emotions. Exactly what was he trying to say? she wondered. For a few ecstatic moments she had hoped he was going to tell her that he loved her, but now she realized that the idea had been wishful thinking on her part. "I've never known how to flirt or act helpless or any of the things that seem to attract a man."

"A man likes for a woman to respond to him. He likes to know she enjoys his advances, that she wants him."

"I always scare off any and all potential husbands."

"I could teach you how to attract men instead of scaring them off. I could teach you what men like and want from a woman." God, was he out of his mind making such an offer? How could he hold her and touch her, instruct her in the art of pleasing a man and then call a halt before actually taking her? How could he give her lessons in lovemaking and then turn her over to another man?

"Are you saying . . . saying that . . ."

"You need to know a lot more about men and women and . . . and sex. You're too innocent, Anna Rose. Some man might take advantage of that, and probably already would have if you weren't such a damned bossy butt."

Placing her hands on her hips, she scowled at him, then in her best authoritarian schoolteacher voice asked, "Are you offering to give me a few lessons? Is that what this is all about? I've done you a favor by letting you stay here and you'd like to repay me by giving me some free instructions on how to snare a husband. Well, thanks, but no thanks. I'd rather die an old maid than accept...charity...from... from you, Britt Cameron.''

Oh, she was angry, he thought. He'd never seen her this way. So, the sweet rose had a few thorns. ''I certainly didn't mean for you to take the suggestion as an insult.''

''Well, I did. I appreciate the fantasy.'' She opened her arms in a mock gesture of gratitude. ''The music, the dancing, the flower.'' She jerked the rose from behind her ear and flung it at him. It landed at his feet.

''What the hell's the matter with you?''

''I want you to leave.''

''Leave the house tonight or leave the farm altogether?'' he asked, shocked by how much her answer mattered to him. He didn't want to leave the farm. He didn't want to lose her as a friend.

''Just tonight.'' She backed away from him when she saw the stormy intent in his eyes. ''You can...can stay on until Corey's able to come back to work.''

He walked toward her. She took several steps backward. He moved again, shoving her gently until he forced her up against the wall. Determined not to allow him to intimidate her, she stared him directly in the eye, but when he lowered his head, his lips almost touching hers, she drew in a deep breath.

With his mouth hovering over hers, Britt said, ''If you change your mind about the lessons, you know where I'll be. Otherwise, I'll see you at breakfast in the morning.''

She didn't move until he'd turned and walked away. The moment she heard the door slam, she sighed and slumped down to her knees. She looked across the room to where a single white rose lay, several loose petals scattered on the floor. Dropping her chin to her chest, she started crying.

Five

Anna Rose gave herself a thorough appraisal in the mirror attached to the back of the bathroom door. She had bought the new blue dress yesterday, telling herself that she really needed a new Sunday outfit. But this evening, she admitted that she'd bought the dress hoping to impress Britt.

Well, she didn't look too bad. At least he couldn't accuse her of wearing something a size too large. Indeed this slender-skirted, padded-shouldered linen dress was an exact fit. Perhaps a little shorter than she usually wore her dresses, but the salesclerk had assured her that the trend was leaning more to above-the-knee styles. Anna Rose wasn't sure what the current fashion was, but did suspect that the dress ended just above her knees due to her five feet nine inch height.

In the ten days since she and Britt had quarreled, she had longed to return to the easy-going friendship they had shared before she had overreacted to his offer. In retrospect, she supposed she'd been hurt because she had fantasized that Britt was beginning to love her the way she loved him. Why had she allowed herself, once again, to want something—someone—she knew she couldn't have? Would she never learn? A man like Britt Cameron, despite his scars and deformed hand, could probably have any woman he wanted. He was so utterly male, so totally, unashamedly masculine. And he was mysterious. She knew little more about him now than she had when she and Lord Byron had rescued him from his wrecked truck.

She had to admit that he wasn't a man to hold a grudge, and he *was* one who kept his promises. When he'd shown up for breakfast the morning after their quarrel, he'd acted as if nothing had happened the night before, but she hadn't been able to pick up where they'd left off. She, not he, had caused the rift in their friendship. She never asked him to stay and talk after meals, and though he tried to be pleasant whenever they were together, she found it difficult not to resent his unemotional attitude.

True to his word, he allowed her to pass him off as her fiancé, backing up her brief, sketchy stories of how they'd met and fallen in love. Whenever they encountered her friends and acquaintances, he let her do all the talking while he simply acted the part of an attentive lover. Those moments proved difficult for her. When he would put his arm around her or give her a hug or plant an affectionate kiss on her cheek, she had to remind herself that it was all for show, that Britt didn't love her and that no power on earth could persuade him to marry her.

People were stopping by the farm, on any pretense, just to meet Anna Rose's fiancé, and whenever she drove into town, to the Piggly Wiggly or the bank or to check on things at school, someone was bound to corner her and ask dozens of questions about her upcoming nuptials. Even Tammy, once over her astonishment that a man like Britt could actually be in love with poor Anna Rose, had stopped by again, offering to give Anna Rose a bridal shower and hinting that she'd be delighted to serve as matron of honor at the wedding.

Anna Rose knew now that she would have been better off if she'd never made up a farfetched tale about having a mystery lover. She supposed she could defend her stupidity by saying that she simply didn't want to look like a fool in front of the whole town. She'd spent her entire life the recipient of everyone's pity. Poor Anna Rose. God, how she hated pity.

But here she was, passing off a stranger as her future husband. A man who'd only be around a couple more weeks. Then what was she going to do? Well, having asked herself that question more than once every day for the past week, she had come to one conclusion. If she couldn't have Britt's love, could never be his wife, then she'd be smart to agree to his offer. Who better to teach her how to be a woman than the man she loved?

Checking her appearance in the mirror one final time, Anna Rose forced a smile on her face. She'd stopped by the store and bought some new lipstick, along with eye shadow and blush. She'd applied all three, then seeing the ghastly sight reflected in the mirror, she'd washed her face and started all over again. Now she wore only the pink lipstick, and a hint of matching blush colored her cheeks.

With a quick detour through the kitchen to pick up the sack of homemade brownies she'd made for Britt as a peace offering, Anna Rose said a silent prayer for strength. If her courage didn't fail her, she was going to walk down to the sharecropper's shack and ask Britt Cameron for a date.

Leaving the top button of his shirt undone, Britt straightened his collar, then ran his hand over his freshly trimmed beard. Taking a long, studious look at himself in the cracked bathroom mirror, he decided he'd done all he could do to make himself presentable. He hadn't really worried about his appearance since Tanya had left him, and he hadn't had a real date with another woman since the car accident more than five years ago.

Well, old son, you don't know that you've got a date to-night. Anna Rose may well tell you to get lost. After all, she'd been less than friendly since he'd made his magnanimous offer to coach her on how to trap a man. Damn, he still couldn't believe he'd been that insensitive. He'd meant the offer as a thank-you for giving him food and shelter and a part-time job, as a sign of appreciation because she'd taken him on face value, never prying into his past, never bombarding him with questions he didn't want to answer. But what he'd done was hurt the one person on earth he didn't want to hurt. She'd taken his offer as an insult. Women! Go figure them.

But he was sick and tired of this armed truce. He wanted things back the way they'd been. He needed Anna Rose's friendship. Despite the fact that he'd sworn he'd never trust another woman as long as he lived, he knew he trusted Anna Rose. She was a rare woman, indeed, and far prettier than she gave herself credit for being. What the hell was wrong with the men in Cherokee? Couldn't they see past the superficial to the beauty that lay beneath?

Well, if Anna Rose didn't want lessons from him about...men and women...about sex, then maybe she would allow him to repay her many kindnesses by letting him show her what it felt like to be courted. From what she'd told him about her past, she'd dated very little before Kyle Ross came into her life and their relationship had never gone beyond hand holding and a few kisses.

Damnation! That was as far as he could let *their* relationship go. But, unlike Ross, he wouldn't lead her on and let her think they might have a future together. In a couple of weeks, Corey Randall would be able to take over his duties around the farm, and Britt knew there would be no reason for him to stay on. He didn't like the idea of leaving, of going back out into a lonely world where the nightmares from his past awaited him. Sooner or later he'd have to return to Riverton, to the accusatory stares and whispers—and to the truth. Someone else had killed Tanya. And Britt knew

that that someone was Reverend Timothy Charles. But
could he ever prove it?

If Anna Rose were a different type of woman, Britt knew
that he would have already bedded her. Hell, they'd be in
the middle of a raging affair right now. He hadn't had a
woman in a long time, and he needed one badly. But the last
thing he wanted was an insecure, inexperienced lover who
was sure to think that sex and love were synonymous. Another woman he could take and leave without sharing any
more of himself than his physical release. Unfortunately he
could never make love to Anna Rose without telling her the
truth about his past. He could never have sex with her, and
then walk away from her in a few weeks.

But he didn't want to leave things the way they were between them. He wanted their friendship intact when he said
goodbye. Who knew, he might want to keep in touch with
Anna Rose, make sure she was all right and even keep tabs
on the men in her life. Sooner or later some smart man was
going to come along and marry her.

With a disgusted grunt, Britt reached down on the sink,
picked up a bottle of after-shave and shook a small amount
into the palm of his hand. He slapped his hands together to
distribute the liquid, then patted it into his beard. He didn't
like the way he felt when he thought about Anna Rose with
another man. Hell, he couldn't be jealous. He didn't love
her. He was just concerned. That's all. She'd been hurt
enough in her life. He didn't want to see anyone else cause
her pain. Anna Rose deserved happiness, and if some other
man could give it to her, then he should be glad.

He'd been thinking about telling Anna Rose the truth, the
complete truth. But why should he burden her with his
problems when he'd soon be gone? What if she didn't understand? What if she suspected he'd killed Tanya? He
couldn't take that chance. When so many people had turned
against him, he had survived despite how much it had hurt.
But Anna Rose's distrust would destroy what little faith he
had left in the human race. He knew she thought of him as

someone special, a sort of rugged gentleman, maybe even a knight in shining armor. Or least she had before he'd opened his big mouth and ruined the unique bond they'd shared.

Well, old son, nothing ventured, nothing gained. In the room he used as both living room and bedroom, Britt removed his jacket from the back of a wooden chair. He slipped on the tan sport coat, wondering if he looked ridiculous wearing it with jeans and Western boots. But he'd packed light when he'd left home nearly a month ago, not ever thinking he'd need a suit.

He headed straight for the front door, stopping just long enough to pull the bouquet of wildflowers from a glass jar filled with water. He'd picked the flowers less than an hour ago, wanting them fresh when he gave them to Anna Rose. She loved flowers, and she was the kind of woman who'd appreciate the gift itself and never the cost.

He had considered buying her a book of poetry, but thought better of the idea. First of all, it would have meant a trip to either Iuka, back in Mississippi, or a twenty-mile drive up to the Shoals area. And second, and more important, he didn't know a damned thing about poetry.

With bouquet in hand, Britt opened the door and stepped out onto the porch. If he were lucky, Anna Rose would accept both the flowers and his invitation out to dinner. And if he were really lucky, she might even forgive him and be his friend again.

They met on the path halfway between her house and the sharecropper's shack. She carried a white sack tied with a red ribbon, a dozen walnut brownies nestled inside. He held a huge bouquet of wildflowers—daisies and tiny pink roses and Queen Anne's lace.

Lord Byron and his friends trailed along behind Anna Rose. The big rottweiler nuzzled Britt's leg. Instinctively, Britt rubbed the dog's head, paying special attention to the spots behind Lord Byron's ears. But all the while he was petting her dog, he was looking at Anna Rose.

They were both utterly surprised by the other's unexpected appearance on the pathway. For endless moments neither spoke. They simply stared at each other.

"Hello." His voice was strong and steady, unlike his nervous stomach and accelerated heartbeat. Anna Rose looked . . . pretty. And she was smiling at him. Well, at least the corners of her mouth were curled and her eyes were smiling.

"Hello, yourself," she replied, then cleared her throat. "How are you?" She'd never felt so quivery inside, and prayed the trembling wasn't outwardly visible.

"I'm fine." He glanced down at the ribbon-tied white sack she carried. "Were you coming to see me?"

Holding out the sack to him, she nodded affirmatively. "I—I made some of those walnut brownies you like so much and . . . and I thought you might want some."

"Thanks. I love 'em. I've never tasted any as good."

The bouquet he held in his right hand caught her attention. "Were you on your way up to the house?"

He thrust the flowers at her. She accepted them with a warm smile. "These are for you. I know they're not much, but—"

"They're beautiful. Thank you."

"Look, Anna Rose—"

"Britt, I'd like—"

Having spoken simultaneously, they both stopped abruptly and laughed. Suddenly neither of them could speak. Only the sounds of Lord Byron and his playmates running through the woods and the rustle of a late evening breeze disturbed the tender quiet. Later, when the sun began to set and the night creatures stirred, the sounds of katydids and frogs and hoot owls would awaken the stillness.

"You first," she said.

"No, ladies first."

"The brownies are a peace offering," she admitted. "I want to apologize for overreacting to your suggestion to tutor me. I'm not used to being the student."

"You don't owe me an apology. I'm the one who's sorry. I like you, Annie Rosie, and I thought that if I could repay you for your kindness by giving you a few pointers on—"

"I know, I know." She took several small, tentative steps toward him. "That's one of the reasons I was coming to see you. I—I've reconsidered your offer."

"You have?"

"Yes. I'd like to invite you to dinner and the movies, and...afterward...well, I'd like to start my lessons." There, she'd said it. The ball was in his court now. The rest was up to him.

"A date?" he asked, moving toward her, never once averting his intense gaze from her face.

"Uh-huh..."

"Would you believe that I was on my way to ask you for a date?"

"You were?"

"I'll drive if you don't mind riding in my old truck. And I'm paying for dinner and the movies."

"Britt, that really isn't necessary. After all, my Blazer is in better condition and I realize you don't have much money. Besides, I know my way around the Shoals. We'll have to go to Florence to the movies, and—"

He hadn't meant to grab her and kiss her, so when he did, it surprised him as much as it did her. It was one of those hard, quick kisses that left both participants breathless.

Holding her close, he rubbed his nose against hers and smiled. "Lesson number one. Don't be so bossy. When a man asks you for a date, assume he's driving and he's paying. Most Southern men are still old-fashioned about stuff like that."

With her heart racing, her knees weak and her breath caught in her throat, all Anna Rose could do was nod meekly. If lesson number two was anything like lesson number one, she wasn't sure she'd live through it.

* * *

By eleven o'clock, they had returned from Florence where they'd eaten at the Court Street Café and later laughed themselves silly at the current comedy hit showing at the Hickory Hills Cinema. They'd run into Tammy and Roy Dean at the movies, and had politely declined their offer to join them at the current adult hot spot in Muscle Shoals. Anna Rose had never been inside a *club,* one of those places her grandmother's generation had referred to as honky-tonks. On the long drive home, she asked Britt about what those places were like, and he'd seemed surprised that she'd never been in one, especially during her college days. She had explained her grandmother's aversion to alcohol and tobacco as well as to music and dancing. Britt's reply had made her laugh.

"Well, to have been such a pious woman, your grand-mother certainly did know a lot about honky-tonks. If she'd never been in one, how'd she know that the places are filled with smoke, loud music and slightly drunk men and women rubbing all over each other on the dance floor?"

Though the interior of his truck had been dark, she was certain he'd winked at her.

Lord Byron, asleep on the front porch, raised his head and gave Anna Rose and Britt a sleepy look, then put his head back down and closed his eyes.

"Won't you come in?" she asked, hoping he remembered that she'd asked for a lesson after their *date*.

"It's such a beautiful night, why don't we sit out here in the swing." He nodded toward the cushioned oak swing hanging at the end of the front porch.

"If you're going to instruct me on men-women relation-ships, we'd have more privacy inside." She wasn't sure what lesson number two would be, but she certainly hoped it would involve more kissing. Britt Cameron had a knack for kissing.

"Hey, lesson number two isn't going to involve anything that we can't do out here." Not that he didn't want to do a lot more than kiss her, he thought, but he'd promised himself that he wouldn't let things get out of hand. "Besides, your nearest neighbor is at least half a mile away. Nobody would know if we stripped off buck naked and chased each other around the house."

Giggling, she punched him on the arm. "Good Lord, Britt, do people actually do stuff like that?"

Slipping his arm around her and guiding her toward the swing, he snarled his lip in imitation of a sinister leer. "People do worse than that, and love every minute of it."

They sat down in the swing, side by side, their bodies touching from shoulder to knee. Anna Rose breathed in the sweet honeysuckle-scented air—pure, Alabama nighttime, country air.

"I'm really going to miss you when you leave," she said, wishing she had the right to ask him to stay.

"I'll miss you, too, Annie Rosie. You're the first woman I've ever been friends with." He squeezed her shoulder.

"You've never been friends with a woman?" *Of course not, you ninny,* she told herself. *A man like Britt would have lovers, not friends, and you're the type a man thinks of as a friend.* She'd had a lot of male friends over the years, but not one lover.

"I'm afraid I've always been a bit macho when it comes to male-female relationships. I tend to think of women as sex objects." He hoped she wouldn't fly off the handle and preach him a sermon on his antiquated, sexist notions.

"In other words, all the women with whom you've had relationships have been lovers and not friends."

"Look, before you get the wrong idea, there haven't been that many women…and there hasn't been anyone in a long time. Not since my wife died."

She spun around so quickly that the movement shook the swing. "You were married?"

"For a couple of years. She, uh, died eighteen months ago." He wasn't sure why, but for some reason, he wanted to share a part of his past with Anna Rose. Even if he couldn't bring himself to tell her about the way Tanya had died, he wanted to tell her about his marriage, about his family and his home in Mississippi.

"I'm sorry, Britt. I had no idea you'd lost someone you loved." Had his wife died in the accident that had left Britt physically scarred and emotionally injured? Anna Rose wondered. And to have gone well over a year without a woman must mean that he had loved his wife a great deal. Perhaps he still loved her.

"I'd known Tanya all my life. Her folks rented and farmed some land in Tishomingo County not far from my parents' farm. We went to school together from first grade through high school." He'd never forget the way just looking at Tanya Berryman had made him feel. She'd been so cute, so perky, so irresistibly helpless and feminine.

"So, you were childhood sweethearts?" Anna Rose hated herself for the jealousy that ate away at her insides. How could she be jealous of a dead woman?

"No, just childhood buddies. She was my best friend Paul's girl, not mine." He'd loved Paul like a brother, had in some ways been closer to Paul Rogers than he'd been to Wade. He'd been careful not to let either Paul or Tanya know the way he felt about her. He'd dated dozens of other girls in school, had learned the earth-shattering pleasures of sex with other women, but he'd never loved anyone except Tanya.

"Oh, well, she must have changed her mind if she married you instead of Paul."

"She married him first."

"She . . . I don't understand."

He'd never talked about his unrequited love for Tanya, not even to Ma or Wade. They'd known, of course, but it hadn't been something they'd discussed. "Tanya and Paul married straight out of high school. I went into the marines. Partly to get away from having to see them so happy and in love—"

"Oh, Britt." She turned to him, overcome by feelings of sympathy, hurting for him, sharing the pain he must have felt in loving someone who loved another. Reaching out, she covered the scarred side of his face with her hand.

He pulled her hand to his lips, caressing the palm with his mouth. "That wasn't the only reason I joined the marines. Pa had died when I was fourteen, and Wade had to take over and keep things running. It was all we could do not to lose the farm. We had two sisters still in school. We needed money bad. I sent home as much as I could. All I didn't have to have."

"What happened to . . . to Tanya and Paul? Did they get a divorce?" Just saying the other woman's name proved painful. Anna Rose had never known such intense jealousy.

He placed her hand against his scarred forehead and held it there. "Five years ago Paul and I had been to a cattle sale and were on our way home. I was driving. We were both stone sober, but tired and eager to get home. I suppose I was driving a little over the speed limit. We had a blowout, skidded, hit a tree. . . ."

When she heard his voice crack with emotion, she wanted, more than anything, to take him in her arms and comfort him, to tell him that she loved him and would always be there to share his sorrows. "You and Paul were in a car wreck," she said, realizing that Paul had not survived the accident. "That's how you got the scars, isn't it?"

"Yeah, but I was lucky compared to Paul. He lost his life." It had been years since he'd cried, and the one time he'd allowed his emotions to overwhelm him, he'd been alone. But right now, with Anna Rose's caring blue eyes devouring him with her love, he had to fight the urge to go into her arms and cry like a baby.

"It must have been so difficult for you . . . afterward."

"I've never gotten over the guilt. I was driving. I lived. Intellectually, I know it was no one's fault, but emotionally I've never forgiven myself for living, for—"

"For finally getting Tanya?"

Britt grabbed Anna Rose, enclosing her within his big, strong arms. She'd never felt as needed, as essential to another person's well-being as she did this very minute.

"You understand, don't you? God, I'd wanted her all my life and the only way I could get her was—" He couldn't say more. Angry tears lodged in his throat, emotions never truly faced before surfaced to torment him.

Anna Rose stroked his back, hoping her touch would ease the tenseness she felt in his tight muscles. "But Tanya must have loved you, too, to have married you."

He held on to Anna Rose, absorbing her gentle strength, comforted by her tenderness. "She was pregnant when Paul died. She miscarried and a few months later tried to kill herself."

"Oh, my God!" Anna Rose tightened her hold on Britt when she felt him trying to pull away. She wasn't going to let him suffer alone. He needed her.

"I married her because I loved her, because I wanted to give her a reason to live. I thought that she'd learn to love me. She didn't." His two year marriage had been a living hell for both of them. He had wanted and expected too much. She'd tried, but she'd never been able to forget Paul. At least not with him.

"How did you lose her?"

"An accident," he said, not wanting to lie to Anna Rose, but afraid to tell her the complete truth. After all, if his suspicions weren't correct, Tanya's death could well have been an accident. Reverend Charles probably hadn't meant to kill her.

She held him in her arms, one hand stroking his back, the other cradling his head where it rested against her breast. His body trembled, and she knew he was fighting the need to cry. Why was it that men were so afraid to cry? Was it really a learned restraint, she wondered, or was it some primitive masculine trait that kept getting passed down in the genes? They sat there in silence, their hearts beating steadily, their breaths coming slowly while the June night surrounded them like a soft, diamond-studded, black blanket. A mild breeze stirred through the trees, issuing a barely discernible melody that somehow wasn't lost in the mélange of woodland music. Nocturnal animals and insects created a symphony heard only in the wild, in the undisturbed, unspoiled places of nature. And a lover's moon floated in the sky, a full moon, lighting the dark night.

She didn't know how long they stayed there, a man and a woman, alone in the world, undisturbed by any living creature. A man in pain, and the woman who comforted him.

She felt him stir and released her protective hold when he raised his head and looked at her. Her heart plummeted to the pit of her stomach. He was staring at her with such hunger, such desperate need.

"Do my scars repulse you?" he asked, but before she could reply he went on. "Or my crippled hand? The scars go down my neck, across my shoulder and over my arm, you know. You've seen them. Tanya hated the sight of me like this. She said my scars reminded her of Paul's death, but I think it was more than that. We never made love with the lights on. We never—"

Anna Rose covered his mouth with the tips of her fingers as warm, heartfelt tears streamed down her face. "I think you are the handsomest man I've ever known. If... if you were mine..."

"If I were yours, what?"

"If you were my lover, I'd kiss every scarred inch and weep for the pain you must have endured. I'd love you all the more for not being perfect." She reached up and kissed his forehead where the ugly scars marred his skin.

Britt couldn't bear the tumultuous emotions brewing within him. It was as if all his feelings for Paul and Tanya— the sorrow over their deaths, the hatred he harbored for Reverend Charles and the misery he'd endured during the trial—collided, and only the sweet, giving entity that held him in her arms could offer him salvation from his torment.

With quick and accurate force, he shot out his right hand, grabbing her by the back of her head, bringing her lips to meet his. His kiss was hard and hot and demanding. As if on command, she opened her mouth to his plunder. And he devoured her. The hunger for a woman had been building inside him, but not for just any woman. He'd been starving for the response of a woman who cared, genuinely cared about him, a woman who wanted him as much as he wanted her.

He couldn't seem to control himself, though reasonable thought kept trying to break through the wild and all-consuming desire that was riding him. While he deepened the kiss, thrusting forcefully into her, he ran his hands over her body... a body so soft and warm and inviting. Taking her hip in one hand, he kneaded her firm flesh with urgent fingers.

She became a willing participant, holding on to him, returning the wild passion of his kisses, longing to do whatever he wanted, but unsure because of her inexperience. Guided solely by feminine instinct, she cuddled closer as a moist heat began to form in the apex between her thighs. When she felt his fingers slowly opening her neck-to-hem buttoned dress, she didn't even consider refusing him.

Her lace-covered breast swelled in his hand the moment he cupped it. Running his other hand up and down her hip and over her tight bottom, he longed to strip away all the barriers between them. When he felt her fingers trembling as she tried to undo his shirt, he released her breast long enough to unbutton several buttons.

"Do you want to touch me?" he asked, his lips on hers, his breath hot and coffee-laced as it mixed with hers.

"Yes." Her answer was part moan and part sigh. The moment he released the buttons, she slipped her hand inside his shirt, curling her fingers through his thick, dark chest hair.

He couldn't hold back the groan that exploded from his throat. Her intimate, yet oh-so-innocent touch ignited a fire of desire within him, a raging inferno of passion. His hand returned to her breast, pinching at the nipple, using his forefinger and thumb to rotate it into pebble hardness. With desperate need eating away at his insides, he pulled her onto his lap and thrust himself up against her as he began again the assault on her mouth.

Anna Rose had never known desire, but she knew exactly what was happening to her. She might be inexperienced, but she wasn't stupid. She had thought this would never happen to her, that she would never feel such raw, primitive hunger. What ecstasy, she thought, to learn what lust was in the arms of the man she loved.

Breaking away, he lowered his head to her shoulder and gave his lips free rein to explore her neck. "I want you, Annie Rosie. I want to make love to you. I want to take you inside and lay you down in that big old antique bed of yours and teach you what it's all about."

"Oh, Britt, Britt, I want that, too." Her heart was so full that she couldn't begin to tell him all that she was feeling.

"Oh, honey. Sweet, sweet, Annie Rosie." No matter how much he wanted her, needed her, he couldn't let her think that he was offering more than a night of passion. She was too fine a lady, too dear a friend.

"Britt, I lo—"

He covered her mouth with the palm of his hand. "Hush. Don't say any more." He lowered his hand, and saw the questioning look in her blue eyes. "I ache with wanting you. But...but I'm not what you need. I can give you tonight and a few other nights, but I can't give you forever, and that's what you want, isn't it?"

He let her draw away from him and reseat herself on the swing. It broke his heart knowing that he had hurt her, but, by being honest, he'd done her a favor in the long run. When she sat there, not moving, not speaking, he wondered what she was thinking. "It's my fault," he said. "I never should have let things go this far. It's just that you're so sweet, so tempting. I'm sorry, honey."

"What if I said tonight and a few more nights would be enough? That if that's all you can give me, then I'll take it?"

"You don't mean that, Annie Rosie. You don't want an affair. You want marriage and children and all that happily-ever-after stuff."

"I want you, Britt Cameron." She looked at him when she said it, dry-eyed and filled with determination.

He cupped her face in his hands, not feeling the least self-conscious about his crippled hand, not with her, not with his Annie Rosie. "And if I could love you, could give you what you really want and need, I'd carry you to bed and make you mine forever." God, how he wished he'd met Anna Rose years ago. Before he'd married Tanya. Before a part of him had died. Before his heart had been buried beneath a layer of pain and bitterness.

"You still love her?" The words were part question, part statement.

"No," he replied truthfully. He kissed Anna Rose softly, tenderly, as if her lips were fragile porcelain and could withstand only the lightest, most delicate pressure. "I don't love Tanya anymore, but she . . . she made it impossible for me to love anyone else . . . ever again."

Releasing her, Britt stood and, with one final farewell glance, walked away. He didn't dare look back. If she was crying, he didn't want to know. It was taking every ounce of strength, every particle of willpower he had to leave her. But she'd be better off without him. He was doing the right thing.

Anna Rose sat in the swing for a long time. She didn't cry. She hurt too much to cry. It was the same way she'd felt when Gramps died. She hadn't shed a tear for weeks.

All she could give Britt was her love, and he'd made it perfectly clear that it wasn't enough, would never be enough, to mend his broken heart.

Six

———

Anna Rose dumped the remainder of her food in the garbage, scraped off the plate and placed it in the dishwasher. She threw her iced tea in the sink. Sunday lunch had been a lonely affair. Her naturally healthy appetite had been spoiled by Britt's absence. She was half tempted to run over to the shack to see if he was still there, but her pride wouldn't allow her to go to him. Surely, she told herself, he'd come say goodbye before he left. No doubt, last night had affected him as much as it had her, albeit in a different way. Being such an honorable man, Britt was probably feeling guilty about what happened.

Anna Rose walked down the hall and entered her bedroom. After Sunday church services, she had come home, thrown off her clothes and slipped into a pair of baggy cotton trousers and a loose-fitting, gauzy top. With meticulous care she now hung up her dress, placed her heels on the shoe tree and put her panty hose and slip in the clothes hamper.

Trying desperately to come to terms with her feelings for Britt, she hadn't slept much last night and had been little more than a zombie at church. Thankfully the lesson she'd prepared to teach the pre-school class was one she'd used in the past. When Tammy and Roy Dean had mentioned stopping by later in the day, Anna Rose had reluctantly agreed. Now she wished she had invented some excuse to prevent their visit. She simply wasn't in the mood to listen to Tammy's prattle.

I wonder what Britt's doing? she thought. And what did he eat for breakfast and lunch? Had he driven down to Cherokee and picked up some canned goods at the Piggly Wiggly? Maybe he'd left during the night. Maybe he'd thought it best not to say goodbye. *Stop it!* she scolded herself. *Stop tormenting yourself. If he's gone, he's gone and there's nothing you can do about it.*

Restless and sick with worry, Anna Rose prowled around the house, looking for something—anything—that would take her mind off Britt Cameron and the way he'd made her feel last night. She loved him, loved him more than she'd thought possible to love someone. But he didn't love her. He had loved his wife, and her inability to return his love had hardened his heart and paralyzed his emotions.

Anna Rose picked up the book of poetry she'd been reading the night Britt had wrecked his truck in front of her house. Slumping down on the couch, she held the book in the palm of her hand. It opened automatically to the page on which Marlowe's poem was printed.

She read aloud the first verse. *"'Come live with me, and be my love, and we will all the pleasures prove.'"* As she continued reading silently, tears formed in her eyes. By the time she neared the last verse, her vision was completely obscured. Closing the book, she quoted aloud from memory the last two lines. *"'If these delights thy mind may move, then live with me and be my love.'"*

So absorbed in the beauty of the words, the depth of the poet's feelings as well as her own, Anna Rose jumped at the sound of loud knocking at her front door. Wiping away the tears from the corners of her eyes, she laid the book aside and went out into the hall.

Praying that her visitor was Britt, she rushed to the door and flung it open. Her anticipation changed to disappointment when she saw Tammy and Roy Dean standing on the porch.

"Are you all right?" Tammy asked. "I was beginning to wonder if something had happened to you. I've been knocking and knocking."

"I—I'm fine. You two come on in." Anna Rose escorted her relatives into the living room. Husband and wife sat side by side on the sofa.

"Where's your fiancé?" Roy Dean asked, turning his round head this way and that. "You should have brought him to church, or ain't he a religious man?"

"Hush up, Roy Dean," Tammy scolded.

"Can I get y'all some iced tea or some coffee?" Acutely aware of the tension coming from her relatives, Anna Rose knew something was wrong. Her cousins weren't paying her a friendly social call. She was sure of that.

"Tea would be real nice." Roy Dean removed his Atlanta Braves ball cap and ran a meaty hand across his partially bald head.

"Don't bother, Anna Rose." Tammy gave her husband a condemning stare. "We...well, we didn't come for a Sunday visit."

"No?" Anna Rose watched the color rise in Roy Dean's fat face. His normal pink-tinted complexion turned a splotchy red. "Then, to what do I owe the honor of this visit?"

"Sweetie, you'd better sit down." Unshed tears misted Tammy's eyes.

Without reply or question, Anna Rose sat in the big rocker near the front windows. Although a virtual kaleidoscope of possibilities raced through her mind, she refused to focus on one specific suspicion.

"It ain't like we want to be the ones to tell you," Roy Dean said. "Hellfire, we're your family. We care about you, and don't want to see you hurt any more than you've already been."

"How much do you know about Britt Cameron?" Tammy stood up and began to pace back and forth in front of the couch, not once looking in Anna Rose's direction.

"What's this all about?" Anna Rose asked, tension rushing through her like floodwaters from a broken dam.

"Where did you meet him? Really?" Tammy asked.

"I told you that we met on vacation last year, that we—"

"You're lying, girlie." Roy Dean's small brown eyes widened to the point where they looked like round shiny marbles set in his face. "We know where Britt Cameron was last year when you were on vacation, and it wasn't with you."

"Hush up, Roy Dean. She probably has no idea what kind of man she's gotten herself involved with." Tammy finally faced her cousin. Lacing together her ring-covered fingers in a prayerful gesture, she gave a theatrical sigh. "I hope you haven't gone and done something stupid, like getting yourself really engaged to him. Tell me that it's all a sham. Tell me you lied about a fiancé to save face after what happened with Kyle."

Anna Rose widened her eyes, her mouth parting in a silent gasp. How had Tammy discovered the truth? And what on earth did she mean about the kind of man Britt was? "You're confusing me. I don't have any idea what you're talking about."

"Me and Tammy both thought the name Britt Cameron sounded familiar." Roy Dean leaned back on the sofa, adjusting his short, heavy body as he buried his wide butt in the cushions. "We didn't figure it out until I was talking to Henry Moss over in Iuka yesterday."

"If Britt Cameron is still around, you'll have to send him packing. As a matter of fact, you probably ought to let Roy Dean ask him to leave. It might not be safe for you to do it.

When I think that the two of you have been alone out here for weeks..." Tammy covered her cheeks with the palms of her hands and shook her head. "No telling what could have happened."

"Hellfire, girlie, you're lucky to still be alive." Roy Dean flopped his flabby arm across the back of the couch.

Anna Rose jumped up, every nerve in her body bow-string tight. "Stop it!" she screamed. "What are you trying to tell me about Britt?"

Tammy grabbed Anna Rose by the shoulders, the shorter woman looking up at her cousin with pity in her eyes. "Britt Cameron killed his wife and they put him on trial for her murder down in Riverton."

Tammy continued talking, but to Anna Rose the words became a blurred buzzing in her ears. The room spun around and around.

"Good Lord, Tammy, she's going to faint," Roy Dean said as he came up off the sofa with rapid speed for a man so heavy. "Move out of the way and let me catch her."

Anna Rose reached out, grabbing the arm of the rocking chair to steady herself. Closing her eyes, she took several deep, calming breaths. Over and over she heard Tammy's words... *Britt Cameron killed his wife... Britt Cameron killed his wife.*

"You all right, girlie?" Roy Dean asked. He stood on one side of Anna Rose while Tammy stood on the other.

"If...if Britt was accused of his wife's murder, why is he free? Are you saying he's an escaped convict?"

"He ain't no convict," Roy Dean said. "Seems the jury acquitted him for lack of evidence."

"But the whole town knows he's guilty," Tammy said. "Henry Moss told Roy Dean that when Britt's wife ran off with the preacher, Britt told anybody who'd listen that if they ever came back to Riverton he'd kill 'em both."

"He was acquitted?" Anna Rose asked.

"That don't mean nothing," Roy Dean said. "The fact is you've been passing off a murderer as your fiancé. Folks in Cherokee are already talking."

"How do they know about Britt?"

"Well, er, that is, I wasn't the only one down at the gas station who heard what Henry had to say. Steve Hendricks was with me." Stuffing his hands into his pockets, Roy Dean looked down at his feet.

"I don't know how you met that man or what possessed you to take in a stranger, but your life has been in danger. Heaven help us, Anna Rose, the man could have killed you in your sleep." Tammy threw her arms around her cousin, giving her a protective hug.

Anna Rose stepped out of Tammy's embrace. "I know y'all came here to tell me this out of real concern for my welfare. Thank you. I'll . . . I'll take care of things myself."

"Oh, sweetie, don't you think you ought to let Roy Dean—"

"No. I'd appreciate it if y'all would go on home. I'm...I'm not afraid of Britt. I can handle things in my own way."

"Do you think that wise, girlie?"

It took her ten minutes to finally persuade Tammy and Roy Dean to leave. By the time she heard their Cadillac pull out of the driveway, she was ready to scream.

Britt's wife had been murdered. He had been accused of the crime. No wonder he was so bitter, so determined not to ever love again. His wife had betrayed him with another man—a minister.

In that moment, Anna Rose hated Tanya Cameron. She hated her for not loving Britt, for betraying him with another man, and, as irrational as it was, she hated her for getting killed and putting Britt through the tortures of the damned. The whole town of Riverton still thought he was guilty, even though a jury had acquitted him. How did that make Britt feel? she wondered. Dear God, she had to go to him, comfort him, tell him that she believed he was innocent. In her heart, she knew that Britt Cameron was not a murderer.

Britt sponged the soapy rag across the hood of his old Chevy, adding more muscle to the job than was actually necessary. The truck wasn't muddy, just slightly dusty, with a sprinkling of dead insects across the front windshield. He needed to keep busy, keep moving, keep his mind off Anna Rose and what had happened between them. Damn it all, how had he allowed himself to get so out of control? The last thing he'd wanted to do was hurt her.

He'd been acting like a coward today, not going up to the house for breakfast or lunch. But he couldn't face her. He couldn't bear to see the pain in her eyes, that soft sad expression. He'd stayed around Cherokee too long as it was, enjoying the friendship, the innocent adoration of a woman who allowed him to keep his secrets, who didn't pry or question him at every turn. He'd taken a lot from Anna Rose—her hospitality, her trust, her friendship—and he had given very little in return. He'd known how vulnerable she was, how needy, and yet he hadn't been able to resist the comfort she so freely offered him.

Grabbing the water hose that lay on the ground at his feet, Britt sprayed the soapy residue off the truck. He knew he'd have to face her, sooner or later. No, he'd have to face her today, he told himself. He had already packed his duffel bag. A man on the run traveled light. But he couldn't just get in his clean truck and drive away. He had to say goodbye. He owed her that much, at least.

He should have gone over for breakfast this morning, gotten all the goodbyes over with, but he'd stayed at the shack and feasted on walnut brownies and strong, bitter coffee he'd brewed on the antiquated hot plate. For lunch he'd opened a can of Vienna sausages and unwrapped some crackers, washing it all down with reheated coffee. Damn, but a man could get used to Anna Rose's cooking. She had a talent for cooking that put even Ma to shame. Hell of waste, a woman who could cook like that with no one to cook for...no man of her own, no kids.

Britt shut off the water at the outside hydrant beside the porch and wrapped the hose into a compact circle before laying it on the front steps. Picking up several rags from where he'd placed them in the bed of the truck, he began rubbing down the metal surface, giving it as much care as he would a prized stallion.

He wanted to postpone the inevitable. He had no idea what Anna Rose would say when he told her he was leaving. Would she be glad to see the last of him, or would she beg him to stay? He had to admit that he wasn't sure which reaction he would prefer.

Anna Rose stood just inside the wooded area along the pathway. The sun hung in the sky like a fiery cinnamon ball casting translucent yellowish light over the earth, brightening the green of the trees and shrubs and thick wild grass, spotlighting the glorious colors of the blue sky and the pink wild roses that grew around the tree trunks and climbed their way upward toward the branches. Honeysuckle, subtly sweet and bucolic rich in its aroma, wafted through the hot summer air. The earlier breeze had died away, leaving a heavy humidity that promised rain by nightfall.

Her mind filled with unanswered questions and her heart bursting with love and compassion, Anna Rose stood, silently and out of sight, while she watched Britt. He was wearing only a ragged pair of cutoff jeans. His bare feet were covered with a light coating of red clay dust. His hair was mussed, as if he hadn't bothered to even run a comb through it. Rivulets of sweat ran down his neck, then through his thick, black chest hair, cascading downward to catch in and be absorbed by the waistband of his jeans where they circled his lean hips.

She wanted to run and throw her arms around him, to tell him that she loved him. She had to face him with the truth he'd been too ashamed to tell her. She understood why he had omitted the past eighteen months of his life when he'd told her about his past. He'd been afraid she'd think he was guilty of murder.

With all the courage she could muster, Anna Rose continued along the path, moving slowly but surely toward Britt.

He heard the crackle of footsteps as they touched the decomposing grass and leaves and broken twigs that cluttered the pathway. Before turning around, he knew who stood behind him. Anna Rose.

What he saw when he faced her wasn't what he'd been expecting. She wasn't smiling, exactly, but she certainly wasn't crying. Her face seemed...serene. Yeah, he thought, she looked as if she were at peace with herself and God on high. And there was something in her eyes—a hint of knowledge that he'd never seen there before.

"Hi." He threw the wet rag on the ground, wiped his hands off on his jeans and gestured toward the house with a nod of his head and a jerk of his wrist. "Care for a glass of water? I could offer you some coffee, but you'd probably take one sip and pour it out."

"I, uh, missed you at breakfast." She forced herself to look directly at him. It hurt. They were making small talk, trying to exchange pleasantries when he was obviously ill-at-ease, and she was dying inside.

"And lunch, too, huh?"

She smiled, but the expression faded as quickly as it had sprung to life. "Britt...I...last night—"

"Damn, Anna Rose, I'm sorry about what happened. It was all my fault. I never should have let things get out of hand that way."

"It's all right. Really. I don't regret last night. It was special, and...and I'll always cherish the memory that you wanted me...even if you can't love me."

He couldn't keep himself from moving toward her, from reaching out and touching her. He took her finger-entwined hands that she held in front of her into his strong, steady grasp. "If I were capable of loving...anyone...I wish it could be you."

"You don't have to say that." His words ripped through her, slicing away her strong resolve not to cry. Powerful, aching tears threatened to cut off her breath.

Bringing her hands to his lips, he placed a kiss atop her folded fingers. "You know I'm going to have to leave."

"Don't...don't go because of my foolishness." The words cost her a high price. She lost the battle to remain unemotional and calm. Tears formed in her eyes. "Stay on, at least another week until Corey comes back."

"I don't want to hurt you. I don't want you to think that there's a chance—"

"No, no, I understand. More than you think I do."

Something in the way she spoke alerted him to the deeper meaning hidden in her statement. Dropping her hands, he took her by the shoulders, his gaze intent on her upturned face. "What do you know?"

"Tammy and Roy Dean paid me a visit after church today. It seems Roy Dean ran into an old buddy of his from Iuka yesterday."

Dread—cold, gut-wrenching dread—spread through him. "And?" He prayed she wasn't about to tell him the one thing he never wanted her to know.

"They told me that your wife had been murdered, and...you had been accused of the crime, put on trial and acquitted." Unchecked tears streamed down her face like the downpour from a slow, steady rainfall.

His grip on her shoulders tightened painfully. He muttered a string of searing obscenities. His topaz eyes turned darker and darker, until they were the color of burnt gold. "I didn't kill her, Anna Rose. You've got to believe me. I hated her for not loving me. I hated her for leaving me. And God help me, I threatened to kill her, but I didn't."

"I know you didn't. Oh, Britt I know you didn't."

He pulled her against him, encompassing her with his strong embrace. She slipped her arms around his waist and hugged herself closer and closer to him. Laying her head on his chest, she began to kiss his naked flesh.

He held her, stroking her hair, anointing the side of her face with his lips. He hadn't realized how much her trust meant to him, how important it was for her to believe him. "She...she left me. Ran off with a preacher. Reverend Timothy Charles. But then, I suppose Tammy's already told you all about it."

She hugged Britt tighter, trying to convey her feelings by her touch, wanting him to know that he could share his pain with her. "You don't have to tell me anything you don't want to. If it's too painful, if—"

He held her as close to him as he could, feeling as if she were his lifeline and without her he would drown in the dark and deadly waters of the past. "I was so angry when she left. I went around spouting off some nonsense about killing her and the good reverend if they ever showed their faces back in Riverton."

"You reacted the way any normal man would have."

"I acted like an idiot." He ran his hand up and underneath the fall of her thick, tan hair, gripping her neck, threading his fingers through the long, loose strands. "When Tanya came back to town, she called and asked to see me. I refused. I told her that we had nothing to talk about. She said that she'd made a mistake and she was sorry. I hung up on her."

"Did you ever see her again?" Anna Rose knew that, even now, on some deeply subconscious level, Britt still cared about Tanya, and that knowledge was like a near-fatal wound to Anna Rose's heart.

"I never saw her alive again." He rested his forehead against Anna Rose's, his breath warm and heavy on her face, his lips trembling above hers. "Damn, I'll never forget the sight of her lying there on the floor in the trailer. I'd been out, down at Hooligans...a roadhouse. I'd been trying to forget about her phone call. I came in, turned on the light and . . . there she was. Lying in a pool of blood. Her blond hair dyed red with her own blood."

Anna Rose felt the beginnings of a tremor as it racked his body, closely followed by another and then another. She held on to him, praying that she could give him strength and comfort and . . . love. "Oh, Britt, how horrible for you."

"I touched her. She was already cold." Another shudder gripped his body. "I called Wade. He came over and phoned the police. I don't remember much of what happened. Wade said that he found me sitting on the floor holding Tanya in my arms."

"It's all right that you loved her, that you mourned her death."

"I didn't cry. Not once, and I still haven't shed a tear."

"Sometimes things hurt too much to cry. I understand."

He eased her away from him just enough to look at her, to clearly see the compassion and trust in her eyes. "How is it that you understand me so well? No matter what I tell you, no matter what you find out about me, you understand?"

"I don't know why it is," she said, afraid to tell him that love had a way of giving a person special insight into the beloved. "The same way you understood about me, my life, my past. Not every man would have taken pity on me and allowed me to pass him off as my fiancé."

"And few if any women would have taken in a perfect stranger and offered him friendship as well as a job."

Although tears still dampened her eyes, she managed to smile. "I guess that makes us a couple of very special people, doesn't it?"

Taking her face in his hands, he stared at her, noting every bone, every inch of flesh, every tiny freckle that dusted the top of her nose. He didn't think he'd ever seen anything as beautiful as Anna Rose, her pink lips slightly parted, her cheeks delicately flushed and her big blue eyes gazing at him with complete love and utter trust. God, he didn't deserve such a woman as this. She was far too good for him. He couldn't give her what she needed, no matter how much he wished he could.

"You're one incredible lady, and you have no idea how wonderful you are." If only the past, his past, didn't stand between them, Britt thought. Finally after a lifetime of loving a woman who, even in marriage, had never belonged to him, he'd found a woman who, with her every look, her every touch told him that she was his—a woman who had never belonged to another man.

"You're trying to say goodbye, aren't you?" she asked, wishing she had the power to erase his past and keep him with her forever.

He nodded, then dropped his hands from her face and stuffed them into his pockets. Throwing his head back and stretching the taut muscles in his neck, he groaned in a rage of anger, damning the powers that be for offering him love when it was too late to accept it. "What are you going to do when I'm gone? How are you going to explain getting yourself engaged to an accused murderer?"

When she reached out for him, he stepped away from her caressing hand. She pulled back, her hurt gaze questioning his abrupt move. "You were acquitted."

"But as long as the real killer is never found, folks are going to think that, in a jealous rage, I knocked Tanya in the head and killed her."

"Surely the police haven't closed the case?"

"I was their only suspect." Britt wondered if she would believe him if he told her who he thought had killed his former wife. "I think Reverend Charles killed her." He waited for a shocked gasp or a word of protest and heard neither.

"She came back to you and he didn't want to lose her. Is that what you think?" Anna Rose realized the assumption made sense. Wasn't it logical that, even a minister of the gospel, who was capable of adultery could resort to violence if he thought the woman he loved wanted to return to her estranged husband?

"I think he followed her to the trailer, they got in an argument and he hit her. I don't think he meant to kill her. It could have been an accident. My lawyer tried to point that out in the trial, that Tanya could have struck her head after a fall instead of falling because she'd been struck."

"Why haven't you told the police your theory?"

"I have. More than once. When they first arrested me. While I was awaiting trial. During the trial. And after I was acquitted."

"Why wouldn't they listen?"

"Because Timothy Charles, despite the fact that he stole my wife, is considered a saint in Riverton. Believe me, the man knows how to control and manipulate people. After Tanya's death, he convinced everyone that she'd left me because of my violent temper. He pleaded for forgiveness and the whole town forgave him." Britt couldn't begin to explain the bitterness he felt whenever he thought about the way Tanya's lover, her probable killer, had used his charismatic personality and his silver tongue to worm his way back into the good graces of Riverton's Christian populace.

"When you leave here, will you go back to Riverton and try to prove your theory?" If only he'd let her go with him, she thought. She'd be willing to give up everything for him, to stand by him and support him until he could prove the truth and free himself from the cloud of suspicion that darkened his future.

"I don't think I'll be going home for a long time. Maybe never."

"Then don't leave, Britt. Stay here." She wanted to say *come live with me and be my love*. Instead, when he seemed about to refuse, she said, "Stay the week, anyway, until Corey comes back."

"Folks around Cherokee aren't going to let you forget that you're harboring a murderer. My staying here could cause trouble for you." He wanted to pull her back into his arms and tell her he wanted nothing more than to stay—for another week, another month, indefinitely. He had begun

to feel relaxed and almost comfortable these past few weeks
he'd spent on the farm with Anna Rose. He didn't want to
give that up. It had been too long since he'd felt at home
anywhere.

"Why don't you let me worry about that," she said,
knowing that she would face the devil himself if it meant
keeping Britt in her life, even if only for another few days.

"I'll stay on one condition," he said, not wanting to hurt
her, but determined to make her realize that they had no
future together.

"When Corey is able to come back to work, I'm going to
leave and I don't want you to ask me to stay." When she
started to speak, he hushed her with his stern look. "I have
nothing to offer you, Anna Rose. Not permanence, not
money, not a good name, and certainly not the kind of love
a woman like you deserves."

She had known, hadn't she, that her dreams were futile?
That what she wanted, she could never have? "Stay the
week. Please." She willed herself not to cry. She was a
strong woman, a survivor. "I promise not to beg you to stay,
no matter how much I'll want to." She stuck out her hand,
palm open. "Deal?"

He stared at her hand, noting the long, shapely fingers,
the square short nails, the slight quivering that signified her
nervousness. "Deal." He took her hand in his and gave it a
hardy shake.

She jerked her hand away. He saw the way her chest rose
and fell with her labored breathing. He knew she was
struggling not to cry again.

"I'll come up to the house for supper, if you'll invite me,"
he said.

"You have a standing invitation," she said. "Don't you
know that?"

"Thanks." He wanted to say more, but knew that nothing he said could change the situation.

"See you about six-thirty, then."

"Six-thirty."

She turned and walked away, not hurriedly, not as if she were running. She didn't want him to think that she wasn't strong enough to give him the friendship he needed without demanding more.

Once deep into the woods, she broke into a run. Hot, heavy tears spilled from her eyes. Her heart wept with the pain of loss; her soul railed against the injustice of life. By the time she reached her house, she was breathless and all cried out. Slumping down on the back porch steps, she reached out her arms to Lord Byron who'd come running the minute he'd seen her enter the yard.

Cuddling the rottweiler close, she nuzzled the side of his head with her nose. "Looks like you're the only male in my life. I had hoped, maybe this time, things would be different, but I was wrong. I guess it isn't meant for poor Anna Rose to have a man of her own."

Seven

Would he stay the week? she wondered. Would they share their meals together, and, afterward, spend hours talking? They had quite a lot in common. Things such as their love for country living, their shared appreciation of life's simple pleasures—sunsets, rainbows, wildflowers. With every conversation, each of them revealed more and more about themselves, about their childhoods, their teen years, their youthful hopes and dreams.

But they had their differences, too. Anna Rose loved poetry and read voraciously, especially fond of romance novels with their inevitable happy endings that life could never promise. Britt didn't appreciate poetry and the only things he read were newspapers, magazine articles and mysteries. He liked to drink an occasional beer; she was a teetotaler. She seldom missed Sunday church services; he never attended.

Anna Rose wandered through the house, the familiar rooms little comfort to her troubled mind and heart. Opening her bedroom door, she stood on the threshold and looked inside. Late afternoon sunshine brightened every corner. Delicate blue-flowered wallpaper created a soft, feminine background for the heavy antique furniture and coordinated well with the white Priscilla curtains that hung at the three long, narrow windows. A blue-and-white quilt, with matching white pillow shams, graced the half-canopy bed.

An overwhelming sense of loneliness swept over her. Would Britt come to the house for supper as he'd said he would? And would he stay the week until Corey was able to return to work? Really, what difference did it make in the long run? Britt Cameron was a temporary man, who'd soon be gone, and she was a forever woman, who'd once again be left alone. In the past she had been able to find solace in her work, her books, and the mundane chores of everyday living. But it wouldn't be that easy this time. She was in love, truly in love for the first time in her life, and nothing could ease the pain of loss she would feel when Britt left.

She sat down on the edge of her bed, clutching her folded hands in her lap as she closed her eyes and uttered a silent prayer for strength. She had so much love to give, yet no one wanted her love . . . no one would return it. A book of poetry lay open on the nightstand. Anna Rose reached out, picked it up and gazed down at the words through a thin mist of tears. *Love. Love. Love.* She hated the very word. Angry at herself for wanting—always wanting—more than she could ever have, Anna Rose flung the book to the floor, then threw herself across the bed, burying her face in the soft, old quilt that smelled of fresh air and sunshine.

Britt knocked on the back door. No answer. For the past hour he'd moped around the shack trying to forget how Anna Rose had felt in his arms, wishing he didn't remember the way she had trusted him, had taken him at his word. There had been no doubt in her eyes, no suspicion in her voice. She had held him, comforted him and listened patiently while he had told her the sordid details of Tanya's death.

He knocked again. Still no answer. Her Blazer was in the driveway, so, unless she'd taken off somewhere on foot, she had to be in the house. He'd met Lord Byron chasing after a stray cat when he'd come through the woods, so he knew she wasn't out strolling with her dog.

Turning the doorknob, he found the back door unlocked. He stepped inside the kitchen, looking around as he made his way across the room.

"Anna Rose."

No answer. Where the hell is she? he wondered. He'd known that she was upset, that she was hurting and had been eager to escape from him. He had wanted to pick her up and carry her inside the shack to the rusty iron bed with the bumpy mattress and threadbare sheets. More than he had needed air to breathe, he had needed the feel of her beneath him, loving and giving and totally accepting. And she would have given him her body, and along with it her heart and soul. But what could he have given her in return except a few stolen hours of physical pleasure? Anna Rose deserved so much more—more than he'd ever be able to give her or any other woman.

Slowly, hesitantly, he entered the hallway, then searched the living room before heading for her bedroom. Had she decided to take an afternoon nap? Had she shut herself off from the world in the privacy of her bedroom and cried herself to sleep?

Just as he reached out, his big hand encompassing the cut-glass doorknob, a loud boom of thunder rumbled overhead. The old Victorian house shook from the force of the impending storm. Opening the door, he glanced inside, and what he saw tore at his heart as much as it aroused every male instinct within him. Primitive urges controlled him. The need to claim what was his, the need to protect, and the desire to mate.

She lay across the bed, her long hair falling wild and free about her shoulders, her face nestled against a pillow, her blouse rumpled and several buttons undone, her legs curled upward and inward in a childlike position. All the way across the room, he could smell the clean, unperfumed essence that was Anna Rose. Soap and water, country air and Alabama sunshine, baby powder and pure female aura. Although he could see only the side of her face, he knew she was crying. He could hear the soft sniffling, the little gasps for breath.

He stood there, unable to move for endless moments as he watched her. He had no right to be in her house, in her bedroom, a voyeur to her most intimate moments of desperation. But he had caused her misery. Wasn't it right that he should take it away?

"Anna Rose." He took a tentative step inside the room.

She jerked around, half sitting, half lying on the bed. Her overbright eyes glared at him, shock and disbelief clearly evident. Her face was damp, her blue eyes swollen and red. Brushing an errant tear from her cheek, she sat up on the side of the bed.

"Britt? What . . . what—"

She couldn't believe her eyes. Britt stood just inside her bedroom, his big body casually attired in the same cutoff jeans he'd been wearing earlier. A short-sleeved cotton shirt covered his chest, but only the bottom two buttons held it together. His feet were bare. His hair, damp and tousled, curled around his ears, several stray locks hanging down over his forehead. She could hear his labored breathing. Had he run all the way from the shack? His strong masculine scent filled her senses. There was an aroma of soap and hot air, of clean sweat and springwater clinging to him. Had he taken a swim in the pond? Had he been naked? she wondered.

"I knocked at the back door. I called out." God, he'd never seen anything as soft and vulnerable and feminine as Anna Rose. And he'd never wanted anyone so badly.

"I didn't hear you." She clutched the front of her open blouse, holding it together with trembling fingers.

"The thunder, I guess." He could see the need in her eyes, the female hunger that tensed her body. "Anna Rose—"

"It isn't suppertime, yet, is it?" She wanted to get up, knew she should stand, invite him into the kitchen and start preparations for the evening meal. But she couldn't move.

"No." She had to know that the last thing on his mind was food. He was starving all right, but his insatiable hunger was for her. "I—I got to worrying about you after you left. I wanted to make sure you were all right."

"Thank you." If he didn't turn around and walk out of her bedroom soon, she wouldn't be responsible for her actions. Unless he wanted to hear her beg, he'd better leave. "I'm . . . okay, I guess. Just . . . just feeling a bit sorry for myself."

"I think you should know that . . . if things were different . . ." How could he say, if you were the type of woman who'd be willing to accept a brief affair, we would already be lovers?

"If I were different." Her voice grew lower and softer, a slight tremor vibrating every word. "If I were pretty and slim and—"

Before she could complete the self-derisive sentence, he had crossed the room, pulled her up off the bed and taken her in his arms, silencing her with his mouth. His lips were hard and moist, his tongue insistent as it plundered, then retreated, only to boldly attack again. She cried out, the sound caught by his mouth as it ravaged hers. No man had ever kissed her this way before—as if he were dying of thirst and she was his oasis in the desert.

She could feel the steady beat of his heart where his chest crushed her breasts. He held the back of her head in one hand, his fingers speared through her hair. He gripped her waist with the other hand, pressing her closer and closer.

Through the haze of intense desire, she tried to think, tried to make sense of what was happening. But rational thought wasn't possible. Not as long as he kept kissing her. Not as long as she could feel the throbbing heat of his arousal pulsating against her stomach. He wanted her, that much she realized. Britt Cameron wanted her. There was no doubt about it. And she wanted him.

Her acceptance of his predatory claim to her body seemed as instinctive as breathing. Slipping her arms, trapped by his possessive hold, around his waist, she worked her fingers up and underneath his loosely hanging shirt. She ran her nails over his tight skin, and gloried in a heady sense of power when she felt him tremble.

Outside, another loud roar of thunder plummeted the summer day, but inside, Anna Rose barely heard the noise, so loudly was her own heart beating.

Britt released her mouth. They both gasped for air. Lowering his head, he looked down to where her blouse hung open, held together by three buttons. He could see her white lace bra, the swell of her full breasts and her dark pink nipples. He placed his mouth against her throat, then slowly made his way downward, his tongue painting a damp, curling line across her chest and into the shadow between her breasts. Anna Rose clung to him, then prompted by urges she didn't understand, she tossed her head backward and thrust her body toward his marauding lips. She spread her fingers out over his shoulder blades, kneading his powerful muscles.

Britt grabbed her by the hips, holding her steady with both hands. He could tell she was melting, slowly, degree by degree, becoming hotter and hotter. When he removed his hands from her hips, she remained locked to him, as if some invisible glue had bound their bodies. She dropped her arms to her sides. Shedding his shirt, he fumbled with her buttons, freeing them, removing her blouse.

Looking at his chest, she could not resist the urge to touch him. A thick, heavy mat of black hair beckoned her fingers. Her hand hovered over his chest. She glanced up at him.

"Touch me." He covered her hand with his, pressing it against his erratically beating heart.

Of their own accord, her fingers inched through his chest hair. She was utterly fascinated by the way the lush dark strands curled about her fingers. "Is this what you want?" she asked, unsure of how to please him.

"That's just a little of what I want," he told her. "Just the beginning."

She watched his head descend, then closed her eyes when his mouth opened over her lace-covered breast, taking a distended nipple and suckling it until she cried out with pleasure. While he lavished similar attention on her other breast, she whimpered, the sound an irresistible inducement to a man who needed very little prompting.

With manic urgency, he unhooked her bra, tearing it from her body. She gulped in huge swallows of air, then flung her hands over her bare breasts with a sudden burst of modesty. His hands covered hers, gripping them, prizing them away from her body.

"Don't cover yourself. I want to look at you."

She couldn't breathe. Her lungs were frozen, her throat constricted. He held her arms away from her body, gazing at her intently, his yellow-brown eyes alight with amber fire. He studied the feminine beauty of her large breasts, so round and firm and irresistible. When he lowered his head again, she made no move to assist or resist. With his hands holding her waist, he made love to her breasts, teasing the nubs with repeated lapping strokes, then tiny, prickling nips with his teeth and finally an all-consuming suckling. She cried out, consumed with aching pleasure.

"Britt, please...it's too much. I can't bear it." She'd had no idea that a man could create such exquisite pleasure inside a woman by the mere touch of his mouth and tongue and teeth on her breasts.

Raising his head, he smiled at her, pleased by the dazed look of rapture on her face. She was incredibly responsive. Lifting her breasts into his palms, he squeezed them gently and felt an almost uncontrollable yearning rip through him when she sighed. The sound was so soft, so passionate, so utterly feminine.

"There's more...much more," he told her, releasing her breasts. He unbuttoned and unzipped her slacks. She made no protest. "Will you let me look at you, see all of you?"

No one had seen her completely unclothed since she'd been a very small child and had been incapable of bathing herself. She had never seen a naked man, and knew at that precise moment that she longed to see him as much as he did her. With a courage derived from a deep internal wellspring, Anna Rose reached out and, with shaky fingers, unsnapped and unzipped his jeans.

He looked at her. She looked at him. "Oh, yes, baby, yes." Britt lowered his cutoff jeans, pulled them over his feet and tossed them aside.

He stood there, big and hairy and thickly muscled. All man. And undeniably aroused. His manhood filled the front of his white cotton briefs. Anna Rose wanted to touch him there, wanted to strip away the one remaining barrier that held his blatant arousal in check.

Without saying a word, he removed her slacks, but when his fingers slipped beneath the elastic waistband of her lacy panties, she panicked and tried to pull away from him.

"Don't, baby. Don't be afraid. I'm not going to hurt you. All I want to do right now is look at you."

While she stood, pliable if not eager, he eased her panties down her hips and over her legs. She raised one foot and then the other. Britt, on his knees before her, laid the scrap of silk and lace on the floor, then buried his face in the apex between her thighs.

Stunned, Anna Rose cried out and would have run from him had he not clutched her buttocks in his hands and held her to him. He breathed in the sweet, musty aroma of woman. He couldn't remember ever wanting anything as much as he wanted to make love to Anna Rose.

When he dampened the front of her thighs with his tongue, she clutched his shoulders, bracing herself. Myriad emotions ran riot within her—desire, so hot and intense it consumed her, diminishing all other feelings. But a deep sense of wonder mingled with an ever present sense of morality. Was what they were doing wrong? How could it be, she asked herself, when nothing she'd ever done had felt so right?

Tormentingly, he moved his lips upward, over her stomach, around her navel, between her breasts and to her throat. Standing upright, he faced her and could see the hint of doubt in her blue eyes. When he pulled her into his arms, she went willingly, her body trembling when his manhood pulsated against the delta between her thighs.

"Britt, please . . . please . . ."

Holding her with one hand at her waist, he ran the inside of his other hand down her cheek, capturing her jaw and chin in his palm. "Do you know what you're asking for?"

"I . . . yes." She closed her eyes, savoring the delicious agony of desire that radiated from her femininity, spreading like the flames of a uncontrollable fire.

"I want you," he said, running his hand down her throat, tightening his fingers, feeling the throbbing of her pulse. "Do you have any idea what I want to do to you?" When she neither opened her eyes nor replied, he said, "Do you?"

She only groaned, lost to the new and painfully erotic feelings that his passionate loving had created deep within her.

"I want to lay you down on the bed." He heard her moan again, a sound soft, but easily detectable. "I want to come down on top of you. I want to bury myself deep inside you. So deep that you'll think I've become a part of you."

When she swayed toward him, he took her in his arms, lifting her off her feet. She knew she was neither small nor light, but he held her as if her size was nothing to him. And perhaps it wasn't, she thought. Britt Cameron was a very large man, with big arms and broad shoulders bulging with muscles.

He laid her on the bed, and slowly eased himself down beside her, propping himself on one elbow as he turned to her. "Have you ever been with a man, Anna Rose?"

The question panicked her. What answer did he want to hear? Did he prefer an experienced woman or would her virginity be appealing to him? "Does it matter?" she asked, so afraid of making the wrong reply. If he left her, walked away now after bringing her so close to the ultimate act of love, she wasn't sure she would survive.

Did it matter? he asked himself. Yes. No. Hell, if she'd never had a man or had been with a dozen, it wouldn't change the fact that he wanted her to the point of madness. "No," he said truthfully, slipping his leg over hers, lifting himself up as he spread her thighs with his knee.

He loomed over her, big and dark and breathtakingly male. She reached out for him. He lowered himself, careful not to crush her, hoping he could take her slowly and carefully, half certain that she was a virgin or, at least, very inexperienced. But the blood rushed through his body, pounded in his head, throbbed in his manhood.

"I don't want to hurt you." He called upon every ounce of his willpower when he probed the moist entrance to her body.

"You won't," she said, curling her arms around him, lifting herself up to meet him. "I trust you completely."

The sweet compliance of her willing body and her total trust in him dissolved the last remnants of his control. He entered her, a fraction at a time. She was hot and wet and tight. So very, very tight. Suddenly he encountered her maidenhead. His whole body tensed with the knowledge of what she was offering him, of what he was taking from her.

"Annie Rosie...Annie Rosie..." With one commanding thrust, he entered her completely, shattering her innocence as he made her his.

She cried out, as much from the fullness, the incredible feel of having him buried deep inside her, as from the pain.

"Baby, are you all right?" He stopped his movements, waiting for her reply.

"Yes, oh, yes. Please, Britt, don't stop. Love me. Love me." She moved first, her seductive feminine body tempting his maleness with a charm she had never known she possessed.

He took her then, in a frenzy that left no room for gentleness or concern for her inexperience. She writhed beneath him, her body answering the primitive mating call of his. Sensation after sensation washed over her as her whole body tightened into one huge, throbbing need. He could feel his own release nearing, and tried to stem the tide of passion flooding him. Lifting her hips, he shoved her up and into him as he lunged in and out, each consecutive thrust deeper and harder and faster than the one before.

With her nails biting into the flesh of his lower back, Anna Rose groaned, overpowered by an intensified ache at the point where their bodies joined. Suddenly that ache became unbearable. Her body tightened.

"Britt, Britt...I love you." She hung on to him for dear life, knowing surely she must be dying, so great was the pleasure, so compelling the tidal wave of fulfillment that consumed her.

"Let it happen, baby. Just hang on tight and let it happen." He could feel her tightening around him, sheathing, stroking.

Ecstasy claimed her. She moaned, then cried out, his name an awed chant on her lips. The sounds of her satisfaction sent him over the edge, triggering the most earth shattering climax he'd ever known.

They stood together in front of the open French doors that led from her bedroom out onto the side porch. Hours ago, the earsplitting thunder and the sizzling lightning had diminished as the heavens opened and rain fell in a hard and furious downpour. Now the rain had turned into a slow, steady shower that would give the earth a deep and thorough soaking.

After they had made love a second time, then slept until twilight, Britt had gotten up and slipped into his cutoff jeans. Understanding her shyness, even after giving herself so unashamedly to him, Britt had retrieved Anna Rose's cotton robe from the closet and turned his back while she slipped it on.

Now she stood in front of him, leaning back against his chest. He draped his arms around her, his big hands lying low on her stomach. He nuzzled the side of her face.

Anna Rose watched the sweet summer rain as it created a sheer haze that covered the earth. "Thank you," she whispered, closing her eyes, savoring the feel of his lips pressing a kiss against her cheek.

"For what?" he asked, wondering if she was thanking him for bringing her to the peak of physical pleasure.

"For wanting me," she said quite honestly.

For wanting her? For wanting her! The loneliness, the emotional deprivation, the low self-esteem came through loud and clear in her words. Had she never been wanted? he wondered. Had that damned old grandmother of hers made her feel so totally unwanted and unworthy that, even now, as an intelligent, successful woman, Anna Rose couldn't imagine someone wanting her? Tightening his hold around her, he buried his face in her long tan hair. God, she smelled good. Sweeter than all the flowers in her garden.

"I've never wanted another woman as much as I wanted you." Although it was the truth, he had been hesitant to tell her. He didn't want her to think that wanting and loving was the same for him as it so obviously was for her.

"Then I . . . I satisfied you?"

"You know you did." He tried to turn her around to face him, but she struggled against the move. "Ah, Annie Rosie, don't go getting all shy on me now."

"It's just that I...I love you so much. Even more now...now that we've made love. And you didn't say the words...you didn't—"

He allowed her to keep her back to him. Placing his chin atop her head where it rested, slightly tilted, against his chest, Britt hugged her tightly. "I wish I could say the words, but I can't. I'd never lie to you. If I said them I'd mean them."

"You still love her, don't you?"

"No," he said. "It's not that I love her, it's just that I don't think I'll ever be capable of loving another woman." When he felt her body tense, he wanted to comfort her, but wasn't sure what he could say or do that would make any difference.

"Will you still be leaving next week when Corey comes back to work?" She held her breath, waiting anxiously for his reply. More than anything, she wanted him to stay. Maybe, if he stayed, he'd learn to love her just a little.

"I don't think so, Annie Rosie." He sighed deeply, calling himself all kinds of a fool. He wasn't some green kid who didn't know better. He'd had no right to put her at risk the way he had, to make love to her without taking the proper precautions. "You realize, don't you, that I didn't protect you. Either time."

"Oh." She hadn't given it a thought, so lost to the new-found joy of being wanted by the man she loved. How foolish! How completely irresponsible! "Britt, I'm so sorry. I—I...I'm sure it'll be all right. I mean, even if I am...that is, I'd never blame you, and I'd never expect you to—"

He whirled her around so quickly that her loosely tied robe fell open, exposing the inner curve of her breasts and the tawny tan triangle of curls between her legs.

"If you're pregnant, I'll marry you," he told her, his tone commanding, leaving her in no doubt of his intentions.

"But...but it wouldn't be right to ask you to marry me. You don't love me. You just said that you'll never love another woman."

"But you love me, don't you, Annie Rosie?" He slipped his hands inside her robe, placing them on her hips, pulling her to him. "And I want you, and respect you, and admire you, and enjoy being with you."

"But you don't love me?"

"No, I don't love you."

The words hung between them, dark and deadly, like a microscopic virus, waiting, waiting, waiting.

Eight

He wore a navy suit, a pale blue shirt and a striped tie. She was dressed in the new sapphire-blue silk suit that Britt had told her matched her eyes. She held a small bouquet of pink wild roses and baby's breath. He had done everything he could to persuade her to wear white, but she had adamantly refused. Perhaps, if he loved her, she would have worn white and felt, since he was her first and only lover, that she deserved the honor. But he didn't love her, despite the fact that she carried his child.

He had stayed with her after Corey had returned to work. He'd tried to find employment locally, but no one wanted to hire an accused murderer, despite the fact that he'd been acquitted of the crime. Anna Rose had defended both Britt and their relationship, not only to Tammy and Roy Dean, but to numerous relatives, friends and even to the county school board.

The past few months had not been easy. When she'd missed her first period, Britt had insisted she see a doctor, but she'd assured him that she was often late and occasionally missed a period altogether. In truth, she'd never missed a period, but she hated the thought that Britt felt trapped, that he was so noble he would marry her without loving her, just to protect her and their unborn child. By the end of the second month, she could no longer deceive herself or put him off. The doctor had confirmed her pregnancy a week ago. Britt had called his family and invited them to his wedding.

Anna Rose, despite the fact that they were marrying because of their child, insisted on marrying in church, with her minister officiating. Britt had balked at the idea, his bitterness toward religion and ministers of all faiths a by-product of his hatred for Reverend Timothy Charles.

Although Tammy had tried her best to dissuade Anna Rose from marrying Britt, she had, once she'd seen how determined her cousin was to go through with the wedding, taken charge.

Two enormous flower arrangements flanked Brother Sherman. Wade Cameron, Britt's older brother, stood at his side, serving as best man. Tammy had insisted on being the matron of honor. The large country church was almost empty, save for Roy Dean, Steve and Edith Hendricks, and two of Anna Rose's older relatives, Opal Palmer and Maude Welborn, both ladies first cousins to her grandfather. Britt's family, except for his youngest sibling Lily, had shown up in full force. His sister Amy had arrived only this morning, but the rest of the Camerons had been in residence since the night before.

Anna Rose liked Wade's wife, Lydia, who had openly discussed her own shotgun wedding, and the happily ever after results. Ruthie Cameron was as good hearted and caring a woman as Anna Rose had ever met, but it was apparent that she didn't completely approve of her son's marriage.

Anna Rose listened carefully to each word Brother Sherman said, repeating the appropriate phrases when called upon, wanting to scream "He's lying" when Britt said yes to the question, "Will you love her and . . ."

Within minutes, it was over. Both she and her husband wore plain gold bands on their fingers, symbols of never-ending love. She barely heard Brother Sherman say, "You may kiss the bride." Britt's kiss was thorough, but quick.

As they turned to step down from the raised pulpit, Anna Rose's head began to spin. She clutched Britt's arm to keep her balance. Slipping his arm around her, he braced her against his body.

"What's the matter?" he asked, concern evident in his voice. "Are you going to faint?"

Taking in several deep breaths as she rested against Britt, Anna Rose shook her head. "I just felt light-headed for a minute. All the excitement, I guess. I'm all right now. Really."

"Could be the heat. This is the hottest September I remember in years," Ruthie Cameron said. "What she needs is to get home and take it easy."

"She can just sit and let us wait on her," Tammy said, making her way to Anna Rose's side. "I've got everything set up at the farm for a lovely little reception. You do feel up to that much, don't you?"

"Of course. I'm . . . I'm looking forward to it. Thanks, Tammy." Anna Rose had been taught, from childhood, that there was a difference in out-and-out lying and telling socially acceptable white lies. Grandmother had been an expert in saying the correct thing, even if she had to stretch, bend or even totally disregard the truth. One never told the complete truth if it injured another's feelings or made one appear foolish in the eyes of others.

When they were outside the church building, Britt helped her into her Blazer. "If you don't feel up to going through with this damned reception, I'll be the bad guy and tell everybody it's off."

"No, don't do that." When she saw the determined look on his face, she smiled and placed her unsteady hand on his arm. "Please."

"Whatever you want, Anna Rose," he said, bending to kiss her on the forehead. "I'm going to try to make life as easy as possible for you. You may not believe this, but I do want you to be happy."

"I know you do." She leaned back against the seat, closing her eyes and willing herself not to cry. Britt Cameron was a good man, the man she loved with all her heart. It wasn't his fault that his own heart was buried so deeply beneath a frozen layer of bitterness and hatred and unrequited love that he was incapable of returning her feelings.

They were married now. For better or worse. They were going to have a child. It was more than Anna Rose had ever hoped to have. But would it be enough—for either of them?

Tammy and Roy Dean had left, taking Opal and Maude with them. The Hendricks had stayed less than ten minutes. Ruthie Cameron had assured Tammy that Amy and Lydia could take care of the cleanup and make sure nothing was left for Anna Rose to worry about.

Anna Rose suspected that her new mother-in-law had been as eager to see the last of the Palmer friends and relatives as she was herself. Opal and Maude had made no pretense of their dislike for Britt, and, although they hadn't been openly rude to him, they had been hostile in their attitude. Roy Dean, a know-it-all big-mouth since childhood, had gotten on everyone's nerves, especially when he'd taken it upon himself to advise Britt to find a way to clear his good name if he ever intended to be accepted in Cherokee.

"Folks around here are going to keep giving Anna Rose a hard time about you," Roy Dean had said. "And when your kid is born, don't think anybody's going to let him forget that his old man was accused of murder."

Tammy, the consummate hostess, at least in a small-town, amateurish way, had flitted around the house like a hyper butterfly, smiling too much, talking too much, and laughing far too loudly.

The evening sun brightened the western horizon, lying low in the sky like some fat, slowly melting scoop of orange sherbert. Anna Rose hadn't changed clothes, but she had slipped out of her heels and put on a pair of flats. Lydia had coerced Britt and Wade and Amy into helping her clean up, while her daughter Molly took baby brother Lee into the bedroom for a nap. Anna Rose suspected that Lydia had maneuvered events in order to give Ruthie Cameron time alone with her younger son's new wife.

Anna Rose sat in one of the big white rockers on the front porch; Ruthie sat in the other. An afternoon thundershower had cooled things off a bit, but had been so brief it had done little more than settle the dust. A few remaining raindrops clung to the shrubbery and rosebushes that lined the front porch.

"We're going to be leaving tonight," Ruthie said. "As soon as little Lee wakes from his nap."

"Y'all don't have to drive home tonight," Anna Rose said, resting her head against the wooden round of the chair as she rocked back and forth, the gentle rhythm soothing to her overwrought nerves.

"It shouldn't take more than an hour. Amy's got a plane to catch tomorrow and Wade's got a farm to run. Two big chicken houses." Ruthie leaned over, placing her fat hand on Anna Rose's arm. "Besides, you and Britt need to be alone on your wedding night."

"It's not exactly as if . . . as if we—" The words lodged in her throat. How could she discuss something so private, so completely personal with her husband's mother, a woman she barely knew?

Ruthie patted Anna Rose's arm gently. "Now, there's no need to be embarrassed around me. Regardless of the circumstances, a wedding night should be special."

"I want you to know that I love Britt, and I'm going to do everything in my power to make him a good wife." Anna

Rose forced herself to face her mother-in-law. "I didn't trap him into this marriage. We . . . we didn't mean for me to get pregnant, and I certainly didn't force him to—"

"Hush up that kind of talk, girl. Nobody's ever been able to force Britt Cameron into doing anything he didn't want to do. He's acted foolishly more than once. Done some stupid things, but his motives are good. For a hot-tempered country boy, he's noble. Yep, that's what my Britt is. He's noble." Ruthie's brown eyes clouded with tears as she reached down to take Anna Rose's hand, squeezing it tightly. "I don't want to see either one of you hurt."

"You know, of course, that he doesn't love me." Just saying the words was a painful act. She didn't know if she would ever again have the courage to voice the heartbreaking fact.

"He thinks he doesn't love you." Ruthie reached up and wiped away the tears from the corner of Anna Rose's eye. "He loved Tanya, had loved her since they was kids, but she was the wrong woman for him. Immature. Selfish."

"We don't always love wisely, do we?"

"Britt didn't. Not the first time, but you're very different from Tanya."

"I'm not petite and blonde and cute." She averted her gaze from Ruthie's disapproving stare.

"No, you're not," Ruthie said bluntly. "You're tall and big-boned, with the kind of body made for hard work and childbearing. The perfect farm wife."

Anna Rose was shocked by her mother-in-law's brutal honesty, not accustomed to people being so truthful. Instead of being offended, she felt a sense of relief that Ruthie hadn't pretended, hadn't sugarcoated the obvious. She couldn't refrain from smiling.

Ruthie smiled back at her, then emitted a sound somewhere between a grunt and a laugh. "God knows you're not cute, Anna Rose. Your features are too strong, your personality too serious. But don't sell yourself short. You're far from being the plain Jane you've convinced yourself you are."

"Ruthie Cameron, where were you when I was a teenager and needed someone like you to talk to?"

Ruthie leaned over and took Anna Rose in her arms, both women half sitting, half standing in their respective rockers. "You give that boy of mine some time. Be patient and understanding, and keep on loving him. One of these days, he's bound to realize how much you mean to him."

"Do you honestly believe that?"

"I know my boy better than anyone else does, and you can take my word for it. Britt loves you. He just doesn't know it yet."

Anna Rose hugged her mother-in-law again and said a quick and silent prayer to a loving God that Ruthie Cameron was right.

Anna Rose had changed into the shimmery white and gold peignoir set that Lydia had given her as a wedding gift. She'd never worn anything like it in her life and felt a bit self-conscious. Britt was still in the shower, had been in there for at least twenty minutes. She couldn't help but wonder if it was possible that he was as nervous as she was. After that first time when they'd made love twice, Britt had assured Anna Rose that he would take care of protecting her when they had sex, but she had told him that she didn't think they should be intimate again. After all, he would be leaving as soon as they were certain she wasn't pregnant, and she admitted to him that it would be far easier to let him go if their sexual relationship didn't continue.

So, here they were, a few months later, married. If only the circumstances had been different, she knew this would be the happiest day of her life. She had longed for someone to love, someone to fill her life with happiness and make all her romantic dreams come true. All her life Anna Rose had longed for a man of her own. Simple little things that other women took for granted had taken on a special significance for her. Just to be able to sit beside the man she loved, to hold his hand, to rest her head on his shoulder. How many times had she wanted and needed a comforting arm around her, an encouraging smile, a caring word or two?

For twenty-seven years she had stored up so much love and so much need. And now she had someone. A husband. At long last, she had found him—that special someone. A man for Anna Rose. But that man didn't love her.

Anna Rose opened the French doors and stepped out onto the side porch. The black night sky was star-studded. An almost full moon released a glimmering silvery-gold light. The smell of honeysuckle and roses saturated the warm summer air.

Hearing the bedroom door open, she turned to see Britt entering. His black hair was damp and beads of moisture clung to the curls on his chest. A blue-and-white striped towel covered him from waist to mid-thigh. Anna Rose swallowed hard, realizing that he was naked beneath the towel.

"The rain cooled things off a bit," he said, wondering what the hell he could do to make things easier for her. This had been a difficult day for Anna Rose, far more difficult for her than for him. After all, he was the one getting everything—a wife who loved him, a child he truly wanted, a chance for a new life. And what was she getting? An unplanned pregnancy. The rebuke and pity of her friends and family. The very real possibility that she could lose her job. And a husband who not only didn't love her, but had a tarnished reputation and no money.

"If you think it's too warm with the doors open, I can turn on the air conditioner." Anna Rose stood in the doorway, suddenly quite aware of how sheer her gown and matching robe actually were. Could Britt see through the almost transparent layers of diaphanous silk?

"No, it's fine. I kind of like the nighttime coming into our bedroom." He began walking toward her, slowly, cautiously, uncertain how she would react to him. After all, for the past two months she had been adamant about not continuing their sexual relationship.

"I imagine your folks are home by now." She turned her back to him, her heart beating wildly. The very thought of his coming to her, touching her, sent her nerves into spasms of expectation. "I really did like all of them. Your niece and nephew are darling. And your mother is such a wonderful woman. I—I wish Grandmother could have been more like her."

Britt kept walking toward Anna Rose, despite the fact that she'd turned from him. Even if they had married because of the baby, even if he didn't love her, Anna Rose deserved a special wedding night. Damn it all, he only hoped he was capable of giving her something. Tenderness, passion, friendship and loyalty. If only that would be enough. "Yeah, Ma's something, isn't she?"

Anna Rose felt him standing behind her, his big body only inches away from hers. Why didn't he touch her? she wondered. Didn't he know that he would have to make the first move, that what little pride she had left wouldn't allow her to initiate whatever was going to happen between them tonight?

"I like the gown Lydia gave you," he said, scanning the length of her body encased in the shimmery white silk edged with pale gold lace. "You look beautiful, even more beautiful than you looked at our wedding today." The moment the words left his mouth, he saw her body tense. Damn! She didn't believe him.

"Thank you." Why did he have to lie to her? she wondered. Her heart might long to hear sweet flattery, but she wanted whatever he said to her to be the truth. She didn't want any lies between them. The one thing they did share was trust in each other, and she didn't want that to change. "Britt, I'd rather you didn't say things you don't really mean."

He moved closer, his naked chest brushing against her back. When he slipped his arms around her and drew her to him, she didn't resist. Lowering his head, he whispered in her ear. "You were beautiful today, and you are even more beautiful tonight. I think marriage and motherhood agree with you."

Her breath came in quick, erratic gulps as he nuzzled her neck. "Please, Britt, I know I'm not even pretty. How can you say that—"

Without warning, he lifted her into his arms, her floor-length gown and robe swirling around his bare legs. "I'll never lie to you, Annie Rosie. Never. When I look at you, I see beauty... pure and honest and real."

She couldn't bear to look at him, so overcome by his adamant profession. Laying her head on his shoulder, she shut her eyes and tried to hold back her tears as he carried her across the room and placed her on the bed.

She lay there, her eyes closed, her heart thundering in her ears, her fingers gripping the quilt. Since he hadn't laid down on the bed with her, she knew he must still be standing. The room was very quiet, except for the faraway sounds of nighttime in the country and the noise of their own heartbeats and breathing. She heard something hit the wooden floor with a light thud, and knew he had discarded his towel.

She felt the bed give slightly from the weight of his big body as he lay down beside her. She wished she weren't so afraid, so uncertain. She knew she could hardly be seductive, lying there like a stick of wood, unmoving and unresponsive. When she felt his fingers touch the tiny covered buttons on her robe, she drew in her breath and held it until he had undone the robe and spread it away from her body.

"This thing is gorgeous," he said, running his hand over the fine lace where it covered her breasts. "But I'd much prefer to be touching your skin than silk or lace."

"I... do you... should I..."

He kissed her closed eyelids while he slipped his hand beneath her back, giving her a gentle push. "Sit up a little, honey, and I'll take care of it."

Obeying like a programmed robot, Anna Rose sat upright in bed and did little more than respond to his requests to raise her arms and lift her hips. The warm night breeze coming in the open French doors struck her naked flesh, puckering her nipples and making her shiver.

With her eyes still closed, she sat there while Britt ran the tips of his fingers from her throat to her navel. An ache began inside her, a tingling, insistent yearning throbbing between her thighs. Her breasts felt heavy and full, hurting with a need to be suckled.

"Open your eyes and look at me, Annie Rosie." His voice, deep and husky, echoed the hot, sensuous longing pulsating through his body.

She didn't respond immediately, but when he dropped his hand below her navel, his fingers slipping through the tan curls to find the moist heat of her body, she moaned and opened her eyes to find him staring directly at her. A warm flush crept up her neck and pinkened her cheeks.

"We can make this marriage work, honey." He fondled her, his fingers moving in a circular motion, creating friction against her damp flesh. Reacting instinctively, she arched against his hand. "I want to make love to my wife."

Nothing, not even her mounting desire, could change the fact that Britt didn't love her, that her whole marriage was based on a pregnancy that neither of them had planned.

"Britt, please..." She grasped his wrist, trying to halt the tantalizing movements of his hand.

Gripping the back of her neck, Britt lowered his face until his lips were almost touching hers. His eyes, bright and glowing with amber brown sparks filled her line of vision. "I know you want me, Anna Rose, so don't try to deny it."

His breath was hot, his lips moist. She gulped down a sob of protest. She wanted to scream, *but you don't love me.* She remained silent, but moved her body toward his, brushing her breasts against his thick chest hair, rubbing her cheek against his beard.

"You don't have any idea how it makes a man feel to know his woman wants him, do you?" He mouthed the question against her lips.

Had his first wife denied him? Anna Rose wondered. Had Tanya Cameron's lack of love extended to a lack of desire? She couldn't bear to think of how much that would have hurt Britt. He was such a proud man, a man of deep and tempestuous passions.

Without giving another thought to denying him, Anna Rose covered his mouth with her own, initiating an intimate kiss. She circled his lips with her tongue, then nipped at her lower lip and finally touched his teeth. He opened his mouth, inviting her entrance.

Like an explosion of the senses, Britt began a frenzy of exploration, moving over Anna Rose, deepening the kiss as one hand continued tormenting her and the other cradled her breast. Placing her hands on his shoulders, she lifted herself upward, inviting him, tempting him. When he nudged her legs with his knee, she opened her thighs to him, offering herself. And all the while she moved her hands over his back, kneading the thick, rippling muscles.

The feelings he created within her kept spiraling, higher and higher, until she writhed beneath him. Breaking the kiss, she gasped for air. "Please, Britt. I want you."

He took her with one powerful thrust. She shivered from head to toe, crying out from the sheer pleasure of their joining. "You make me feel the way a man wants to feel." His words came from him in a thick, heavy drawl as he plunged in and out of her with quick, deep stabs.

She clung to him, reveling in his complete possession. Britt might not be in love with her, but he was loving her body with total obsession.

Slowing his pace, he ran his lips down her throat and to her breast. She squirmed when he took her nipple between his teeth, nipping, then licking, then nipping again.

She accelerated the rhythm of her upward lunges, intensifying the sizzling friction building between her legs. It hit her, wild and hot and all-consuming. "Britt...Britt...love you..." she screamed out into the stillness of her bedroom.

Her fulfillment sent him over the edge. Her tight body surrounded him, clinching and releasing him as spasm after spasm of release quivered through her. His big body jerked once, twice, and then he groaned, a loud and animalistic roar, signifying his completion.

When he lay down on top of her, she cradled his sweaty body in her arms, loving the feel of his damp hairy chest against her breasts, the earthy manly smell he emitted through every pore of his body, the satisfied grunts he continued to make. And most of all, she loved the feel of him still inside her, a part of her, as surely as the child he'd given her.

Easing off her and onto his side, he cradled her head on his shoulder, then kissed the side of her face. "Thank you."

"Thank you," she said, cuddling closer, knowing that in the future she would never deny Britt her body, that despite the fact that he didn't love her, she did love him.

And maybe, just maybe, Ruthie Cameron had been right. Maybe Britt loved her, but just didn't know it. With that thought uppermost in her mind, Anna Rose closed her eyes and slept until dawn, when her new husband awakened her and took her to heaven once again.

Nine

Anna Rose took her coat out of the hall closet. From where she stood near the front door, she could hear the sound of the Blazer's motor running and the chilling wail of a below-freezing December wind. She slipped into her coat, not surprised that it barely buttoned across her protruding stomach. Some women, she knew, didn't even show at five and a half months, but already her body had expanded, her belly rounded like a big balloon. A large baby, Cousin Opal had said. Too much water retention, Cousin Maude had decided. But Tammy had probably guessed correctly. Anna Rose was just eating too much and would probably be as big as an elephant by the time she delivered.

Anna Rose set her wool-felt beret on her head, tied her scarf around her neck and pulled on her gloves. She didn't want to keep Britt waiting. He'd had the Blazer running for at least ten minutes and was now waiting on the front porch in the windy cold. They'd had another little disagreement, which they always had whenever she asked him to go any-

where in Cherokee with her. She didn't blame him for
wanting to avoid the curious stares, the behind-the-back
murmurs, and the out-and-out confrontations with the few
people brash enough to question him about his first wife's
murder.

Tonight was the annual Christmas play followed by the
PTA party to honor the school staff. It was one of the most
important events of the year for Anna Rose. She wanted her
husband to share the night with her, and didn't think it too
much to ask that he did. After all, she'd completely given in
to his wishes to stay on the farm. He hadn't gone into
Cherokee more than four times in the three and half months
they'd been married.

Anna Rose opened the door and stepped outside, shutting her eyes momentarily before sucking in her breath as the
frigid night air swirled around her.

"Come on," Britt said, taking her by the arm. "Let's get
you in the Blazer before icicles form on your nose."

Within seconds she was seated inside the toasty warm
four-wheel drive. Britt backed out of the driveway. Neither
of them said a word for a couple of miles down the road.

"I appreciate you going with me tonight. It means so
much to me." She reached out and touched him on the arm.

He shrugged off her tender gesture. "Folks aren't going
to be pleased that you've brought me along." He looked
straight ahead at the desolate patch of darkened country
road ahead of them. His resistance to attending this event
had more to do with his desire to protect Anna Rose than his
desperate need to avoid being the center of attention.

She didn't know how to reply. What could she say? She
couldn't tell him that he was wrong. The past few months
had not been easy for either of them. With each passing day,
she became more and more aware of her friends' and relatives' disapproval of her marriage, and the fact that the
school board president's wife had implied that Anna Rose's
job could well be in jeopardy hadn't set well with Britt. He'd
threatened to go and have a personal talk with President

Davenport. Anna Rose couldn't go anywhere without having to confront the whispers, the stares, the pointing fingers and the blatantly rude behavior of people she'd known all her life. The words *poor Anna Rose* had taken on new meaning.

And matters had only worsened during the Thanksgiving holidays when the Cameron clan had come to Cherokee. Everyone had enjoyed the gathering, and Anna Rose had been in her element for days ahead, preparing a scrumptious feast. But before the Camerons left, Wade had taken Britt aside to inform him that Timothy Charles had found a new church in nearby Iuka, Mississippi. Britt had told Anna Rose that his brother had advised him to quit running from the past and try to clear his name by proving Reverend Charles's guilt.

"He's right," Britt had said. "You're suffering because of my reputation. And our child will suffer even more if he has to go through life having people think his father is a murderer."

"But, if the Tishomingo sheriff won't even consider Reverend Charles as a suspect, what can you do?" she'd asked him, half afraid that if he did go after Timothy Charles, he would leave her and never come back.

Britt had admitted he didn't know what to do, but that soon, he'd have to make a decision.

Anna Rose rested her head on the back of the Blazer's front seat, wishing that she and Britt could run off to some deserted island where no one knew either of them, where they didn't have past lives. When they were together alone at the farm, life was good. They were quite compatible, enjoying each other's company and finding shared pleasures in the simplicity of their daily lives. And when they made love, Anna Rose could almost forget that her husband didn't really love her.

Howard Gene Dowdy, in his new crisp overalls, plaid shirt and baseball cap stood by the punch bowl talking to Kyle

Ross, who looked his usual debonair self in brown slacks and a camel sport coat.

"Rudolph the Red-Nosed Reindeer" played over the intercom and hordes of costumed youngers milled around the school lunchroom, spilling Kool-Aid punch and dropping cookie crumbs over the shiny linoleum floor. Parents of various ages, sexes and races mixed and mingled while a small group of rather superior mothers, those with *important husbands,* detached themselves from the others. Several of those important husbands were busy ogling Nina Costairs, the curvaceous young kindergarten teacher who had bent over to help tie one of her student's shoelaces.

Anna Rose, trapped between Myra Davenport, the school board president's wife and Tracy Ross, Kyle's skinny blond bride, scanned the room for a glimpse of Britt.

"My dear, it's a pity you're showing so quickly," Myra said. "People are such gossips. They'll be implying all sorts of things. After all, you do look ... well ... huge."

"I think you look lovely, Mrs. Cameron," Tracy said, smiling pleasantly at Anna Rose. "Pregnancy certainly agrees with you. You're just glowing."

"Thank you, and please call me Anna Rose." She'd tried to dislike Kyle's wife, but it was impossible. Tracy Ross was sweet and friendly and very likable.

"I thought the Christmas play was a huge success, didn't you, Mrs. Davenport?" Tracy asked.

"Well, I have to admit it's the biggest crowd we've ever had." She tilted her salon-coiffured head and stuck her snobbish hawk nose into the air as she surveyed the multitude of Cherokee parents and grandparents as well as numerous aunts and uncles. "No doubt, the possibility of your husband's appearance here tonight prompted the curious to come out in such frigid weather."

Anna Rose had to bite her tongue to keep from making an acid reply. The word frigid would have been the cornerstone of her comment. Instead, turning to Tracy Ross, she chose to ignore Myra's stinging barb. "I understand that you and Kyle have bought the old Vickery place."

Tracy picked up the conversation and after a few minutes of being completely ignored, Myra Davenport walked off in a huff. "Obnoxious woman," Tracy said, then laughed with Anna Rose.

Britt had tried, unsuccessfully, to disappear into the woodwork, seeking dark corners and spots near exit doors for the past hour. He'd seen Anna Rose scanning the cafeteria more than once looking for him, and hated himself for leaving her on her own. But he figured she was better off if he wasn't by her side gaining them both undue attention.

The after-play party seemed to be winding down a bit, quite a few guests having already left. He noticed Anna Rose talking to Kyle Ross and his wife, and wondered how Anna Rose felt about the couple. Ross was certainly a good-looking devil and his petite wife was the physical antithesis of Anna Rose. Tracy Ross was wide-eyed immaturity packaged in a doll-like body.

Britt decided he'd delayed the inevitable long enough. Making his way across the room, he stopped dead still when he heard Howard Gene Dowdy's loud, nasal voice uttering a comment about Anna Rose.

"Sure never figured an old maid like Anna Rose would go and get herself married to a murderer." Howard Gene hooked his big, fat thumbs beneath the straps of his overalls and stuck out his barrel chest. "Of course, I guess a desperate woman will settle for getting a little anywhere she can."

The group of three men standing around the punch bowl joined the loudmouth in his bellowing laughter. Turning around, Britt accidently ran into a matronly lady who took one look at him, gasped and moved quickly out of his way.

"Now, if I'd known Anna Rose was looking to put out, I'd have offered myself." Howard Gene laughed again, egged on by the receptive response from his listeners, who themselves made a few unflattering remarks about Anna Rose.

"Hell, yeah, I could've had her back when we were in high school, but I didn't figure she was the type, you know." Howard Gene was too absorbed in his ribald comments to notice that his comrades weren't laughing, that they were slowly backing away from him. "We ought to ask ol' Kyle. Bet he could tell us what kinda—"

Howard Gene wasn't able to finish his sentence. A huge hand gripped him by the neck. Another equally strong hand clutched his shoulder. And a pair of fiery amber eyes issued a warning. "You sorry bastard." Britt tightened his hold around Howard Gene's thick neck. "My wife happens to be a lady. And the next time you open your mouth to say anything about her, you'd better remember that fact."

Howard Gene's big round eyes bulged, startling blue in contrast to his bright red face. He tried to pull loose from Britt's tenacious grip.

"Hey, man, you're choking him," one of the other men said. "Give him a chance to apologize, will you. Howard Gene didn't mean no offense. Everybody knows he's full of—"

"Britt!" Anna Rose called out, rushing across the room. The remaining crowd parted, allowing her to pass.

"Do something, Anna Rose. Your husband is going to kill Howard Gene," a bespectacled, red-haired Clayburn Davenport pleaded. "Howard Gene didn't mean those things he said about you. It was just men talk. Nobody meant for your husband to hear."

"Britt, please let him go," Anna Rose said.

Britt hesitated for a few seconds, wanting nothing more than to beat the living daylights out of the foul-mouthed moron. Slowly he relaxed his hold around the man's neck, then released him altogether. "Remember what I told you."

Britt turned his back on Howard Gene, hoping he could explain his actions to Anna Rose so that she would understand and forgive him for putting her on public display the way he had.

"Britt, look out!" Anna Rose shouted.

Britt whirled around just in time to see Howard Gene draw back his meaty fist. Acting on instinct and the practice he'd gained in more than one roadhouse fistfight, Britt landed a hard blow to Howard Gene's midsection, followed by a solid right cross straight into his jaw. Like a mighty timber, Howard Gene fell to the floor, the loud thump echoing in the deadly stillness of the cafeteria.

Britt glared at the people standing around staring back and forth from him to a horizontal Howard Gene, a mixture of awe and fear in their eyes.

"We're leaving," Britt said, grabbing Anna Rose by the arm and practically dragging her across the room, through the murmuring crowd.

"I can't let things go on this way," Britt said, throwing his shirt on the bed. "We can never have a life here in Cherokee as long as people think I killed Tanya."

Anna Rose sat on the bed, her arms clutched possessively around her expanded waist. What had happened tonight had brought their lives to a turning point. All the months of hoping people would accept Britt, accept their marriage and allow them to live some sort of normal life had vanished. After what Britt had done to Howard Gene, no matter how justified, folks would say that Britt's actions were evidence of his hot temper—the same temper that supposedly led him to kill his first wife.

Stripping off his shoes, socks and jeans, Britt turned out the overhead light and sat down on the bed by Anna Rose. "I know you're still upset about what I did."

"I could lose my job. One of those calls we had before I took the phone off the hook was from Kyle. He said that after we left, Myra Davenport preached poor old Clayburn a sermon on the kind of example I was setting for the children."

"I'm sorry." Britt reached out, pulling up the cover as he lay down beside Anna Rose. "I did what I had to do."

"I know Howard Gene was going to hit you . . . and I realize he must have said some pretty awful things about me, but—"

"When we go to Riverton for Christmas, I'm going to talk to the sheriff again, see if I can get him to do more than give lip service to keeping the investigation open." Feeling her withdrawal, Britt wanted to pull her into his arms and tell her that she had no reason to feel threatened by his memories of Tanya. He didn't love Tanya anymore. He didn't even hate her now.

"I'm tired, Britt. I think we should try to get some sleep." She turned over, clutching the covers up to her neck.

He lay there for a long time thinking about what had happened tonight, about how much Anna Rose was having to endure because of him. He couldn't let her go on suffering because he'd been too much of a coward to face the past and finally put it to rest. He owed her more than this, and he damn well wanted his child safe from all the ridicule he and Anna Rose couldn't escape.

His child. Growing inside Anna Rose's body. He reached out and placed his arm around his wife, resting his open palm over her belly. When she tensed, her body tightened and the child gave a sturdy kick.

Britt nuzzled Anna Rose's neck. She lay silent and unmoving. "I'm sorry, honey. I never meant to do anything that would hurt you."

She released a long, deep sigh and covered his hand with her own. "I know."

"I wanted a child with Tanya." He felt Anna Rose go rigid. "No, honey, don't do that. Don't tense up when I mention her name. What I felt for her is no threat to you, to our marriage."

How could he say that? Anna Rose wondered. By his own admission he had loved only one woman in his entire life, and because of that woman's inability to return his love and her subsequent betrayal, he could never love again. Unable to respond verbally, Anna Rose simply squeezed his hand, pressing it down against her stomach.

"You're the best thing that ever happened to me. You know that, don't you? You've given me so much." Slipping his hand out from under hers, he ran the tips of his fingers upward until they encountered her swollen breasts. He circled her nipple through the thin layer of her much-laundered, cotton-flannel nightgown. She sucked in her breath.

She knew he wanted her. He always wanted her. The problems with their marriage didn't lie in their bed. The one constant between them was their unbelievable sexual compatibility. But how long could sex without love keep them together?

"I'm going to find a way to make all this up to you." With one hand caressing her breast and the other easing her gown up her thigh, Britt whispered raw love words into her ear.

By the time his fingers delved beneath her tight curls, Anna Rose dripped with desire. When Britt slid his briefs down his legs and kicked them to the foot of the bed, Anna Rose snuggled backward against his heated arousal. He lifted her leg slightly and positioned himself, easing into her sheathing warmth. With slow, rhythmical motion, he set the pace for a gentle, leisurely lovemaking. All the while he moved in and out of her with such savage tenderness, he stroked her breasts, paying special attention to her overly sensitive nipples. With her neck arched, her heart soaring and her body throbbing, Anna Rose swelled and tightened around him, trembling when his knowledgeable fingers fondled her sex.

On the verge of fulfillment, Anna Rose quivered and reached out, clutching the side of his hairy leg. And then ecstasy claimed her, shivering through her body. While still experiencing climactic aftershocks, Anna Rose cried out her love. Britt accelerated the pace of his thrusts, faster and harder and deeper. Release poured out of him, hot and furious. Shuddering, he hugged her to him, whispering her name.

Hours after Britt fell asleep, Anna Rose lay awake. Easing out of bed as quietly as possible, she reached for her robe lying at the foot of their bed. The house held a wintery nighttime chill. She slipped into her robe and slippers, then walked out into the hall.

When she entered the living room, she felt her way in the dark until she reached the switch Britt had rigged up when they'd put the lights on the Christmas tree. She flipped the switch. Hundreds of miniature white stars sparkled on the eight-foot pine tree.

She stood back, away from the tree, watching the tiny lights flickering on and off in the darkness. Her child moved within her, secure and loved, safe in his mother's womb. More than anything she wanted to give her child the things she had never had. Two parents. Love. Understanding. Self-confidence. Security.

During all the lonely years she had devoted herself to her career, she had dreamed of a husband and child of her own. How strange, she thought, that one's fondest dreams could come true and still not bring happiness.

Lord Byron walked up beside her, nuzzling her leg with his nose. She bent down and rubbed his head. "Couldn't you sleep, either? What's wrong? Problems with your love life?"

Anna Rose sat down on the couch, curled her feet up beneath her and gazed at the tree, remembering all the Christmases her grandmother had refused to indulge in the foolish luxury of a Christmas tree. After Grandmother died, Anna Rose had put up a tree every year.

Lord Byron opened his enormous mouth in a yawn as he stretched his big body and lay down at Anna Rose's side. "I love him so much," she said. "But you know that, don't you, big boy. And so does he. But no matter how much I love him, I can't make him love me back."

Britt found them at two o'clock in the morning. Anna Rose asleep on the couch, her ever-faithful rottweiler asleep beside her. Tiptoeing across the room, he pulled an afghan from the back of the couch and covered Anna Rose with it. Lord Byron opened his eyes, cocked his head and looked up at Britt.

Britt patted the dog on the head and smiled. "It's all right, buddy, you know I'd never hurt her." The moment he whispered the words, Britt knew them for a lie. The very fact that he'd become a part of Anna Rose's life had hurt her, and as long as he didn't resolve the unsettled issues from his past, he'd go on hurting her.

Ten

___

Britt whipped the zipper closed on his nylon gym bag, but left it lying on the bed. He crossed the room to where Anna Rose stood by the window, her back to him.

"Maude will be here before dark. She said she was looking forward to taking care of you for a few weeks." Britt placed his hand on Anna Rose's shoulder. She lowered her head, resting it on his hand.

"You can't promise me that you'll come back in a few weeks." *I will not cry,* she told herself. She had already exhausted her supply of tears, as well as patience, the past few days while she'd been pleading with Britt to let her go to Riverton with him.

"You're right, I have no idea how long this will take." He placed his crippled left hand on her other shoulder and nudged her backward.

She pulled away from him, turning slowly to face him. "I know that you're doing what you think is right, what you feel you must do. But...but I need to be with you. Can't you understand how I feel?"

"I don't want to leave you. Especially since you're over six months pregnant." His amber eyes pleaded for understanding. Hesitantly he reached for her, relieved when she allowed him to take her into his arms. "But you know we'll never be able to live a normal life until I can prove, beyond any doubt, that I didn't kill Tanya."

"I understand. I accept the fact that you have to go back to Riverton, but I could go with you." She clung to him, fighting a tremendous battle to hold back the tears that were smothering her.

"You can't afford to take a leave of absence from your job." He stroked the long, plaited braid that rested on her back, easing his hand downward to caress her waist. "That's all Myra Davenport would need to finally badger her husband into asking for your resignation."

"I could speak to Clayburn, explain—"

"No. You know it wouldn't do any good. He could promise you anything, but once you were gone, that viper-tongued wife of his would stay at him night and day. I can't ask you to give up anything else for me. You've spent years building your career. I've already taken your good reputation from you, I won't be responsible for ruining your career, too."

"I know you're doing what you think is best for all of us, you and me and the baby." She gave him a tight hug, then pulled away. "You'd better be on your way if you want to make it to Riverton before dark."

Running his hand down over her large stomach, Britt cradled the bulge that was his child. "I'll call every day to check on you and my little quarterback." He leaned over and kissed her, tenderly, possessively, then released her and turned away.

She watched him put on his heavy sheepskin-lined jacket and pick up his gym bag. He stopped in the bedroom doorway.

"I'll miss you, Annie Rosie."

She smiled although her heart was breaking. It was all she could do not to run after him, begging him, one final time, not to leave. But she simply stood there in the quiet of the bedroom that had given her sanctuary from the world since she'd been a child. Gray shadows floated across the floor, creations of fading afternoon sunshine.

She heard the old Chevy truck's motor start, listening as Britt backed out of the driveway. Lord Byron's low, plaintive howl came from the living room.

Well, that was that, she thought. Nothing she could do but accept the fact that Britt was gone, for God only knew how long. His return to Riverton had been brewing since Thanksgiving, and she was surprised that he had waited this long.

All of his explanations for leaving her behind were perfectly logical, and her mind accepted them without question. But her heart was another matter. Her emotions told her that Britt's return to Riverton would renew all his memories of Tanya—the good as well as the bad. Even though Britt had convinced himself that he no longer loved his former wife, Anna Rose wasn't so sure. Britt Cameron's emotions ran deep. He was a passionate man, and once he loved, he would love forever.

Even if Britt could prove that Reverend Charles killed Tanya, would that set Britt free to love again? And, even if it did, who was to say that he would ever love her?

Britt waited in the truck, the lights off and the motor not running. The cold January wind was beginning to seep inside the cab, and despite the fact that he wore his heavy coat, his rabbit-fur-lined gloves and his brown Stetson, he was damned cold. How much longer could choir practice last? he wondered. Peering down at his expensive lighted digital watch that Anna Rose had given him for Christmas, he saw that it was almost nine o'clock.

He'd spent the past two weeks in Riverton, talking daily to the sheriff. Hell, not only talking to him, but harassing him. The authorities hadn't seemed the least bit interested in a former accused murderer's suspicions about a beloved minister. Hoping to discover any possible evidence, Britt had sought out people he had once avoided, people who had known Tanya and hated him because they believed him guilty of her murder. But he'd gained nothing except a renewed bitterness and complete frustration. To make matters worse, he missed Anna Rose. He'd gotten so used to her. To her smile, her laughter, her companionship, and the pleasure he found in her body.

Suddenly the church doors opened, flooding the front steps with light. Britt scooted down in the seat, and, peering over the steering wheel watched while members of the Iuka Congregational Church's choir said their farewells, got in their cars and drove away. One man stood alone on the front steps, waving goodbye, a wide, charismatic smile on his handsome face.

Britt flung open the door and jumped out of the truck. Walking at a fast trot, he crossed the street, rushing up the steps just in time to catch Reverend Timothy Charles before he closed the church doors.

Reverend Charles looked at Britt with startled blue eyes, then gave the doors a hard push, trying to close them in Britt's face. Britt reached out, grabbing the door while he inserted his foot over the threshold.

"You wouldn't be trying to shut out a poor sinner on a cold night like this, would you, Reverend?"

Britt gave the door a hard shove with his shoulder. Timothy Charles moved backward when Britt stepped inside the foyer.

"What do you want, Cameron? Why are you here?" Timothy's tall, slender body stood outlined against the darkness of the sanctuary behind him where only the lights illuminating the baptismal were burning.

"I heard you'd found yourself a new church here in Iuka." Britt watched the other man carefully, wondering why he'd never noticed before how much Timothy Charles resembled his one-time best friend Paul Rogers. It wasn't so much that their facial features were identical, although Paul had possessed the same pretty-boy looks. No, it was more in coloring, fair-haired and blue-eyed, and in the long, lean body structure. Was that why Tanya had fallen for the good reverend? Had she seen the resemblance? Had she pretended Timothy was Paul?

"The fine Christian people here, in Iuka, in Riverton, are willing to accept my repentance and give me a second chance." Despite the cold air blowing in from the open doors, sweat dotted Timothy's brow and moistened his upper lip. He twined his long, slender fingers together in front of him in a prayerlike gesture.

"You're a lucky man. You seduced my wife, ran off with her, then killed her, and people are willing to give you a second chance." Britt resisted the overwhelming urge to put his hands around Timothy's neck and choke him until he confessed the truth.

"I didn't kill Tanya! I loved her . . . and she loved me." Timothy backed into the sanctuary, slowly, one step at a time. "She never loved you, but you wouldn't let her go. She didn't want to hurt you, but she didn't know what else to do."

"Then why did she come back to Riverton? Why did she call and ask to see me?"

"She wanted a divorce."

"Did she? Lawyers could have handled a divorce. No, that wasn't why she came back." Britt reached behind him, slamming the front doors, twisting the heavy metal lock until it clicked.

When Britt turned around, he saw that Timothy had backed himself halfway down the darkened center aisle in the sanctuary. "If you leave now, Cameron, I won't report this to the police." The man's voice, so strong and commanding in the pulpit, now sounded like the whimper of a frightened little boy.

"There's nothing to report." Britt started walking down the aisle toward Timothy. "You're a minister. Your job is to comfort those in pain, administer to sinners in need of your help. I'm a man whose life has been destroyed, and you're the one person on earth who can help me."

"I'm warning you." Timothy held his arms up in front of him, his palms spread wide as a signal for Britt to stop. "No one is going to believe anything you say when it's your word against mine."

"Tanya was leaving you, wasn't she?" Britt asked, slowing his stride when he was within several feet of Timothy. "It took her six months, but she finally realized you weren't Paul, didn't she?"

"She wasn't coming back to you!"

"No, she probably wasn't, but more than likely she was coming to me for help, the way she'd done all her life. I was her friend a long time before I became her husband." Britt took several tentative steps forward until he stood chest-to-chest with the reverend. "Was it an accident or did you mean to kill her?"

"I didn't . . . I . . ."

Just as Timothy started to bolt, Britt grabbed him by the shoulders. "I'm back in Riverton and I'm going to stay until I can prove who really killed Tanya. I'm close by, and I'm going to be watching every step you make. I'm going to be breathing down your neck from now on."

"You're insane. I'll call the police and have you arrested." Timothy struggled to free himself, but found his captor's hold far too strong.

"I don't think you want to stir up trouble, do you, Reverend? I'm the one who wants people to start thinking about Tanya's murder, to start talking about the hows and whys and whos again. I'm the one who's determined to prove that you killed my wife."

Britt shoved Timothy Charles backward. The minister hit the red-carpeted floor with a resounding thud. Britt stared down at him. "Just keep in mind that, not only is God watching you, but so am I."

Britt turned and walked away, his hands trembling, his heart beating like a trapped beast within his chest. He had to get away from Timothy Charles before he knocked the truth out of him, and that was something he couldn't afford to do. He had to bide his time and wait for the good reverend to make the next move.

Four days after his nighttime encounter with Reverend Charles, Britt was no closer to unearthing the truth than he'd been when he first arrived in Riverton nearly three weeks ago. Although he spent part of his days helping Wade out around the chicken houses, his nights were spent alone.

Britt lay on the bed in the trailer, the bed he had never shared with Tanya. After being gentle and patient and understanding the first few months of their ill-fated marriage, Britt had finally given up trying to give his wife pleasure. She had accepted him into her body, but she had never responded. After the first year, he seldom touched her. He had loved her, but he hadn't been able to bear making love to her knowing she was thinking of Paul.

Being married to Anna Rose had shown him what a farce his first marriage had been. What he had with her was real. She loved him, only him, and accepted him for the man he was. But what had he given her? Did she ever wonder if he thought of Tanya when...

"Hell!" He sat upright in the bed, appalled that he'd never even considered the possibility that Anna Rose could have thought he compared her to Tanya. Perhaps, when they'd first met, he'd noticed the differences in their looks and personalities, but after getting to know Anna Rose, he realized that she was a woman beyond compare. Every other woman, no matter how beautiful, paled beside Anna Rose. Even his memory of Tanya.

And never once when he'd touched Anna Rose had he thought of his first wife. When he wanted Anna Rose, she filled his senses so completely that she was the only thing in his world.

He had called her thirty minutes ago and had been surprised that there'd been no answer. He'd tried not to worry, telling himself that Maude would have called if anything was the matter. He'd just wait another hour or so and call again. His nightly phone conversation with Anna Rose was the only thing keeping him sane. Being back in Riverton, surrounded by memories, angered by the lack of cooperation he'd received from the sheriff and tormented by the fear that he might not ever be able to prove his innocence, Britt felt overwhelmed by the pain and bitterness that had driven him from his hometown nearly eight months ago.

What he needed was a drink. Maybe he should hop in the truck and run over to Hooligans for a couple of beers. But what would Anna Rose think if she found out, and he'd tell her when he called her. He and his wife didn't keep secrets from each other.

Coffee. Hot and rich and served with a slice of Anna Rose's apple pie. Only he couldn't make coffee that tasted like his wife's and her apple pie was fifty miles away in Cherokee.

Damn, but he missed Anna Rose. Her smile, her laughter, the dreamy expression on her face when she was reading poetry, the way she talked baby talk to Lord Byron—the way she came into his arms whenever he wanted her and filled him with a man's pride.

Just as he took the jar of instant coffee down from the cabinet in his tiny kitchen, he heard the sound of an approaching vehicle. It sounded like a four-wheel drive, Anna Rose's Blazer to be exact. By the time he'd made his way into the living room and flung open the front door, she was standing on the bottom aluminum step.

"Anna Rose." If he didn't know for sure that he was wide awake, he'd swear he was dreaming. He'd wanted her with him so badly, he could easily have conjured her up. "God, woman, get in out of the cold."

He stepped down and practically dragged her inside the trailer, then helped her off with her coat, beret and gloves before taking her in his arms and nearly squeezing the breath out of her.

Her large, rounded belly kept him from acquiring the intimate contact his body craved, but just the feel of her in his arms was more than enough.

"I couldn't stay away any longer, Britt. Three weeks." She threw her arms around his neck and smiled up at him. "I started to call, but I was afraid you'd tell me not to come, so I surprised you."

"You're a wonderful surprise, Annie Rosie." Lowering his head, he kissed her, tenderly, almost reverently. She was the most precious thing in his life, and he just now realized it. "I wouldn't have told you not to come."

"Really?" She hadn't known what kind of reception she'd receive when she arrived, unannounced. Britt had been so adamant about her not coming to Riverton with him that she'd been uncertain how he would feel about a weekend visit.

"Really." He kissed her again, a bit more forcefully, but still couldn't get her body close enough to his. "My son is in the way." Britt covered her stomach with both hands. "Three weeks and he's grown. Are you sure there aren't twins in there?"

"Dr. Middleton says one very big boy."

"Come on, honey, sit down and rest. You must be tired after driving all the way from Cherokee."

"It's only fifty miles." She didn't resist when he led her to the couch. After seating her, he shoved a round ottoman beneath her feet. "Oh, Britt, I need to go get my suitcase. I left it in the Blazer. And there's a sack with some walnut brownies, a half gallon of chicken stew and an apple pie I baked this morning."

"I'll get it all later. It's as cold as an icebox outside so the food won't spoil."

"But I'll need my gown—"

"The trailer is toasty warm. You won't need anything but me to keep you warm." He sat down beside her and drew her into his arms, lifting her onto his lap.

"You've missed me." Sitting sideways, she cuddled against him.

Unzipping her corduroy jumper, Britt ran his hand inside and around to fondle her breast still covered by a turtleneck cotton sweater. "That's the understatement of the century."

Working with hurried but gentle hands, Britt removed her clothing. First the jumper, then the sweater, followed by her stockings and shoes. When she wore nothing but her bra and panties, he picked her up and carried her into his bedroom.

When he laid her down on the unmade bed and began tearing out of his own clothes, Anna Rose sat up and looked around the room. Britt threw his jeans into a nearby chair, then stopped before removing his briefs.

"This is a two-bedroom trailer. This was my room. When I slept with Tanya, I went to her room." He nodded to the wall behind him.

"How...how did you know—"

"Because I used to wonder about Paul all the time." When he saw her flinch, he wished he could rephrase his statement. "Every time I touched Tanya, I knew she was thinking about Paul. That knowledge chipped away at my manhood a little bit at a time. I was a fool for ever marrying her."

"The two of you had separate bedrooms?" Anna Rose asked, surprised by his admission.

"Sex for Tanya and me wasn't very good." He sat down on the bed, taking Anna Rose's chin in his hand, gripping tenderly. "It was never anything like it is between us, so don't think that I've compared you to Tanya or our lovemaking to... When I make love to you, Annie Rosie, there is no other woman on earth.''

''Oh, Britt.''

''Hey, now, don't cry.''

''I'm sitting here as big as a barrel, overly emotional about everything and feeling so alone and unwanted, then you go and say something like that...and make me feel...feel...''

Still holding her chin, he lifted her face to his and planted a quick, wet kiss squarely on her mouth. ''Did it put you in a romantic mood?'' he teased.

Easing away from him, Anna Rose unhooked her bra and dropped it on the floor, then lifted herself just enough to remove her maternity panties. ''If you're interested in making love to a very pregnant woman, I know one who's available.''

While he stripped off his briefs, he never stopped looking at her as he smiled devilishly. ''This is going to take some figuring out. I've never had to devise a plan to maneuver lovemaking around a ten-pound tummy.''

''I'm open to suggestions,'' she said, spreading her legs apart as she lay down.

''Oh, you hussy. What am I going to do with you?''

''And here I thought you were a man with vast experience.''

''Annie Rosie, with you, every time is a new experience.'' He had never missed anyone or anything the way he'd missed his wife. Her love had turned his life around, given him hope where he'd had none, joy where he'd only known sorrow, laughter where he'd only known bitterness.

While she touched him and whispered words of love, he began a thorough worship of her body, his hands and lips and tongue learning every inch of satin flesh as he gave back to her a portion of the pleasure she'd given him in the months since he'd first made her his.

Her normally large breasts were very full, the aureoles darker, the nipples bigger and already producing occasional drops of milky white liquid. Soon his son would nurse at her breasts. The thought sent a surge of pure masculine urgency through him. From her neck to her heels, Britt covered her with tender strokes and moist kisses. Aware of her breasts' ultrasensitivity, he took extra care when he caressed them, dying with the need to be inside her when she moaned with pleasure.

"You're so beautiful pregnant," he told her, his lips pressing a series of adoring kisses across her stomach. "I think I should just keep you this way."

She laughed, then sighed, running her fingers through his hair as his lips traveled beyond her navel and anointed the thatch of thick curls. When he spread her legs farther apart, she made no show of protest, only whimpered as his mouth touched her intimately.

"Britt—" she finally managed to say.

"Don't talk. Don't think. Just enjoy."

And she did. With every stroke of his tongue, every tight caress of his lips, Britt brought her closer and closer to the edge. Thrashing her head from side to side, she squirmed as she clutched the bed sheets. He took her breasts in his hands, raking his thumbs back and forth over her nipples until he felt her convulse, once, twice, and then her whole body shook with release. He continued his loving until he knew she was spent.

While Anna Rose came to terms with the tiny ghosts of sensation that still warmed her body like embers left over from a raging fire, Britt eased her onto her side, pulled her back against his chest and slowly entered her. After only a few hard, quick thrusts, fulfillment claimed him.

Turning to gaze lovingly into his warm eyes, Anna Rose cuddled against Britt. "Every time I look at you, I'm glad that I'm a woman."

"Ah, Anna Rose, what a thing to say to a man." He kissed her, then enfolded her in his possessively tender embrace.

They went to sleep that way, both of them naked and sated, Anna Rose wrapped securely in the arms of the man she loved.

Eleven

Britt awoke abruptly. He looked over at Anna Rose, curled against him and sleeping peacefully. Other than his wife's gentle breathing and the thumping of his own heart, the only sounds he heard were the moaning of the icy February wind and the purr of a car's motor.

A car? In his driveway at this time of night? Jumping out of bed, he reached down on the floor for his jeans, slipped into them and headed straight for the front door. He opened the blinds covering the glass door just in time to see several bright red spots disappear into the darkness. A thin layer of frost covering the glass and the pitch blackness of predawn obscured his vision. He couldn't see the make or model of the vehicle leaving his drive, but by the size and shape of the brake lights, he guessed his unexpected visitor drove a late-model car.

But who the hell would have turned off a country road and driven a quarter of a mile up a private drive to simply turn around and leave? It didn't make sense.

A cold chill shivered through Britt, more a result of unwanted suspicions than from the weather. Returning to the bedroom, he checked on Anna Rose, who still slept soundly. He dressed quickly, wanting to check on things outside. The minute he opened the front door, the strong acrid scent of smoke engulfed him. And then he saw the fire. The wooden lattice work that flanked the underpinning of the trailer burned with a quickly spreading flame.

What the hell? Who? Why? Anna Rose! Thinking of nothing but his wife, asleep inside the trailer and totally unaware of the danger that threatened her life and their unborn child's, Britt ran back inside, racing to the bedroom.

Flinging the covers off Anna Rose, he wrapped her in a quilt. She awoke with a start when Britt scooped her up into his arms.

"What's wrong? Britt..."

"You're safe, honey. You're safe," he said as he rushed through the trailer, stopping only long enough to retrieve his truck keys from the coffee table.

Using his booted foot, he kicked open the front door. A gush of wind blew the rising flames into his face. Jerking around to prevent the fire from touching them, he realized that they couldn't escape by this route.

The back door! God, he had to get her out before the rapidly spreading fire reached the heating-oil tanks on the north side of the trailer. He knocked open the door. Although smoke billowed from beneath the back steps and Britt could see orange sparks floating in the black sky, the path was clear.

Running, he made his way to his old Chevy truck, opened the door and shoved Anna Rose inside. He jumped in, slamming the door behind him. With shaky fingers, he inserted the key in the ignition. The motor rumbled, spluttered and coughed.

"Damn it, start you..." Britt let out a stream of obscenities as he pumped the gas pedal.

"Oh, my God, Britt." Anna Rose sat, clutching the quilt around her, feeling the frigid night air that seeped through the cracks in the old truck. "How...how did the trailer...?"

With a few choice words, half curse and half prayer, Britt tried again to start the truck. He realized that Anna Rose had no idea how close they were to death. If he couldn't get the truck started before the fire hit the fuel tanks, the explosion would rip through the truck and . . . Start! Damn it, start. The motor growled and sputtered. If it didn't start this time, they'd have to make a run for it, out into the fields. But Anna Rose could hardly run in her condition and just how fast could he run carrying her?

Looking out the windshield, he saw the flickering tongues of the orange-gold blaze licking at the fuel tanks.

The motor turned over, starting with a roar of protest. Britt rammed the gearshift into reverse. With lightning speed, he backed the truck up the long drive. Just as they reached the country road exit, a powerful explosion rocked the trailer, sending fire and smoke shooting into the heavens.

Anna Rose screamed. One long, uncontrollable cry. Britt put the truck in park, then pulled Anna Rose's trembling body into his arms.

"It's all right, honey. We're safe." He kissed her forehead, her eyes, her cheeks, her mouth, her chin. He ran his hands over her from neck to hips, stopping to pat her round stomach. "I think all the excitement woke up my little quarterback."

"Oh, God, Britt, how can you joke at a time like this? We could have been killed. Your trailer is gone. My Blazer is on fire. My clothes are in there . . . and the food I brought you . . . and . . ."

He covered her mouth with his, swallowing her words and putting a stop to her lengthy tirade. Anna Rose might be sitting naked and wrapped in a quilt, she might have come within an inch of losing her life, but she certainly hadn't lost her spunk. God love her, she was priceless.

When she began struggling, he released her. She sagged into his arms. "We need to call the fire department," she said.

"I'll take you on over to Wade's place and call from there." He tucked the quilt across her breasts, his big hands gentle as he tightened them on her shoulders, reassuring himself that she was really all right.

"But . . . but I don't have on any clothes."

"Lydia and Ma will find you something to put on."

"Oh, tarnation. What will your mother think?"

"She'll think you sleep in the buff." Britt couldn't keep from smiling.

Emitting a shrill wail of anger and aggravation, Anna Rose muttered, "Double, triple tarnation."

"Why don't you just go ahead and cuss? No matter how much you'd like to let out with a few hells and damns, all you ever say is—"

"Grandmother never allowed ugly words to be spoken in her presence, so just shut up, Britt Cameron, and take me to Lydia's so I can put on some clothes before I freeze to death."

Mile after mile of four-lane highway stretched ahead of her. The sun had set, leaving less than thirty minutes of daylight, but Anna Rose knew she'd have no problem making it home before dark. She was only a few miles outside of Cherokee, just having passed the Allsboro turnoff.

Her surprise visit to Britt two nights ago had turned into more of a surprise than she could ever have imagined. She hadn't wanted to leave Britt, especially after the fire. But he had insisted that she return to Cherokee, telling her that she would be safer at home, and that he wouldn't have to worry about her while trying to prove Reverend Charles's guilt.

The sheriff and the fire department determined that the fire had been deliberately set. They had spent a big part of Saturday sifting through the debris that had once been Britt's trailer. When Britt suggested they question Timothy

Charles concerning his whereabouts, the sheriff gave Britt a skeptical response and even suggested that he might have set the fire himself to try to discredit the good reverend.

Britt's whole family was worried, but they backed him one hundred percent. They all knew that Britt could never lead a normal life until Tanya's real killer had been brought to justice. But everyone was realistic, especially Ruthie Cameron, who'd voiced her opinion to Anna Rose this morning.

"The only way this whole mess can come to an end is if Reverend Charles confesses. It's been over two years since Tanya died and he seems to be able to live with his conscience."

Suddenly, Anna Rose knew what she had to do. Britt's strategy was to shadow Timothy Charles until the man couldn't stand the constant scrutiny, but, if Reverend Charles had set the fire that destroyed Britt's trailer, then who was to say that he would stop short of murder—again?

At the next median crossing, Anna Rose turned her rental car around and headed west. The Sunday evening church services were well under way by the time she pulled up in the Iuka Congregational Church parking lot.

Realizing she might appear a bit conspicuous in the maternity jeans and red flannel shirt she'd borrowed from Lydia, Anna Rose slipped into a back pew and removed the brown wool coat that Ruthie had loaned her.

The choir finished singing "Whispering Hope." Reverend Charles approached the microphone. He was an extremely attractive man, almost femininely beautiful. And the moment he began to speak, utter quiet descended upon the congregation. Even the children and crying babies seemed mesmerized by his strong, authoritarian voice, his theatrical actions and his charismatic presence. No wonder people refused to believe this man capable of murder, Anna Rose thought. One would sooner accuse the angel Gabriel than this man of God.

The contrast between Timothy Charles and Britt Cameron became so evident in Anna Rose's mind that she could easily see why the good people of Riverton had accused the wrong man. Britt's dark, surly looks, his scarred face and crippled hand, combined with his hot temper and bitter attitude, painted a picture of a devilish roughneck.

When the lengthy service ended and people milled about in the vestibule, Anna Rose spoke only when spoken to, informing the friendly church members that she was visiting from Cherokee. Biding her time by looking at the bulletin board, she waited until the last of the crowd had gone outside before speaking to Timothy Charles, who stood just inside the open front doors.

"Reverend Charles?" She paused directly beside him.

"Sister, we're so pleased to have you as a guest tonight." His smile beamed like a three-hundred-watt bulb.

"Reverend, I have a personal problem, one I desperately need to discuss with you."

"Of course, Sister, of course. Just let me close these doors against the cold." His task accomplished he turned back to Anna Rose. "We can talk in the sanctuary or we can go to my office."

"The sanctuary will be fine."

He followed her. She sat down in the last pew in the center row. "Now, my dear, how may I help you?" He sat beside her.

"It's my husband." Anna Rose prayed that she wasn't making a mistake, that by coming here tonight, she wouldn't push Timothy Charles into another violent act.

"Yes, how can I help your husband?" He covered Anna Rose's hand with his own.

It took every ounce of her willpower not to jerk away from him. Anna Rose thought the man's disarming personality was lethal. How could poor, unhappy Tanya have resisted such practiced charm? "My husband was accused of a crime he didn't commit."

"How terrible for both of you, but I believe a good law-yer would help you far more than I could. Unless, of course, you've come to me for prayers."

"I've come to ask you for the truth."

Timothy's clear blue eyes widened suspiciously. "Who are you?"

"I'm Anna Rose Cameron, Britt's wife."

Dropping her hand abruptly, he stood. "I had no idea Britt had remarried."

"As you can see," Anna Rose said, patting her stomach, "we're going to have a child. Although Britt was acquitted of Tanya's murder, he can't go on with his life while the real murderer goes free."

"I see he's filled your head with all his lies about me." Timothy shrank back against the wall. His voice quivered. His hands shook. He grabbed the back of the bench as he gazed at some invisible point beyond Anna Rose's vision. "If you love your husband, then you must convince him to end his vendetta against me."

Anna Rose saw the fear, raw and ugly, on the reverend's face, and she knew in her heart that Britt was right. This man, for whatever reason, was responsible for Tanya's death.

"Someone set fire to Britt's trailer early Saturday morn-ing. We could have died, Britt and I and our unborn child."

"I had no idea that you—"

"Was it an accident?" Anna Rose asked. Standing, she took a couple of steps toward Timothy. "Tanya's death *was* an accident, wasn't it? You never would have deliberately harmed her."

"I loved Tanya." His eyes glazed over with memories, his voice low and soft, almost a whisper. "She was sunshine and light, truly one of God's perfect creations. We didn't in-tend to fall in love. I was helping her with problems in her marriage."

"She never loved Britt." Anna Rose heard the front doors open, but noticed no sign of awareness on Timothy's face.

"No, she never loved him. She didn't want to hurt him. Neither of us did. But life with him became intolerable for her."

"So, she came to you and you took her away," Anna Rose said.

"Yes. What else could I have done? I loved her and she needed me."

"But she came back to Riverton after six months and called Britt, begging for him to see her."

Anna Rose's breath caught in her throat when she looked at the center aisle entrance into the sanctuary. With his hair tousled from the wind and his sheepskin-lined jacket hanging open, Britt stood beside a middle-aged man wearing a uniform. Neither Britt nor the sheriff made a sound.

"I don't suppose you ever knew Paul Rogers, did you?" Timothy asked, tears forming in his eyes. "He was the only man Tanya ever loved. Not Cameron. Not me. I could have gone on pretending ... but she couldn't. She left me."

"Was she coming back to Britt?"

"No, she ... she just wanted to talk to him, ask his forgiveness and try to make things right. She didn't want either of us." Tears streamed down his face. He gripped the back of the bench so tightly that his knuckles turned white.

"Tanya went to Britt's trailer, but he never saw her alive," Anna Rose said. "Tell me what happened."

Britt took a step into the sanctuary. Anna Rose gave him and the sheriff, who was right behind him, a warning look. They stopped dead still.

"I followed her to Cameron's trailer," Timothy said. "She planned to wait for him. We argued. I begged her to come back to me. I told her that I could accept the fact that she loved Paul, that I was willing to act as a substitute for him."

"But she refused, is that it?"

"Do you have any idea how it feels to love someone who doesn't love you?" Timothy fell to his knees on the carpeted floor, laid his head on the velvet-cushioned bench and wept like a heartbroken child.

Anna Rose went to him, placing her hand on his head. "Yes, I know," she said.

Timothy gazed up at her, his face pale, his eyes swollen and red. "She told me to leave, to go back to the congregation and ask their forgiveness. She told me she was sorry for everything."

"How did she die, Timothy?" Anna Rose kept stroking his hair. He turned his face into her belly and clutched the back of her knees. "God knows you didn't mean to hurt Tanya. He understands."

"I grabbed her by the shoulders, begging her . . . pleading with her. When . . . when I tried to kiss her, she slapped me. I reached out...I shook her. She...she fought me...jerked away and fell. She struck her head."

"It's all right, Timothy, it's all right." Anna Rose comforted him, feeling more pity than any other emotion toward the man who had put her husband through a living hell for the past two years.

"It was that antique flat iron she used as a doorstop." Timothy released Anna Rose, seating himself on the bench. "There was blood. So much blood. All over the floor and in her hair . . . her beautiful blond hair."

Britt stepped forward, taking Anna Rose in his arms. Timothy Charles seemed oblivious to everything and everyone around him. The Tishomingo County sheriff read the reverend his rights, then handed him over to the officer who had been waiting in the vestibule.

"I'll need a statement from both you and your wife, Mr. Cameron," Sheriff Jett said. "We'll get everything done up nice and legal so we can take care of Reverend Charles. I'd say he's going to need a doctor as well as a lawyer."

"Thanks," Britt said, then turned to Anna Rose, taking her by the shoulders. "What the hell did you think you were doing coming here and confronting Charles alone like that?"

"Why are you here?" she asked, sticking out her chin defiantly.

"Don't answer my question with a question. Do you realize what a stupid thing you did? For all you knew, Timothy Charles could have killed you."

"He didn't. Now, please explain why you and the sheriff showed up?"

"It seems Sheriff Jett finally had to take my accusations seriously when a couple of witnesses came forward to say they'd seen Reverend Charles's white Mazda come barreling out of my drive around three o'clock Saturday morning."

"Who?"

"Jimmy Skinner and Danny Collier, a couple of boys who'd been to Hooligans and were on their way home. They didn't think much about what they'd seen until they heard about my trailer burning down. They heard it from Jimmy's ma, who picked up the gossip at church this morning."

Anna Rose took in a deep breath, then released it slowly. "Thank goodness this is all over. After we make our statements to the police, I just want to go home and sleep for a week. I'm exhausted."

"Exhausted!" Britt reached out for her, but she ducked his grasp.

"I came here tonight hoping that I could—"

Britt captured her upper arms in his viselike grip. "You put your life at risk, and the life of our child. The good reverend is mentally unstable. What do you think would have happened if the sheriff and I hadn't shown up?"

"I don't know. Not for sure. I—I have to admit that I hadn't thought everything out. I just acted on impulse. I wanted to do something to help."

"Woman, you need a keeper."

"I most certainly do not." She yelped when he lifted her into his arms. "Put me down. I'm perfectly capable of walking."

"Shut up, Annie Rosie, before I really lose my temper."

She had slept from the time her head hit the pillow at ten o'clock that night until Ruthie Cameron had awakened her with a breakfast tray at eleven the next morning. The entire Cameron family had treated her as if she were made of spun glass, especially Britt, who had ranted and raved until his fiery temper burned out and he finally lay down beside her and held her through the night.

Facing Britt had proved to be difficult, exceedingly difficult. For she had made a decision that both of them would have to live with for the rest of their lives. After everything that had happened, she realized that, despite how much she loved Britt, if he didn't love her, they had no hope of real happiness.

Britt deserved to be happy. And, tarnation, so did she. His reaction had been exactly what she'd expected. He had not made any sudden confession of undying love. He'd simply pointed out that they were married and expecting a child.

"I'm leaving this afternoon," she'd said. "I'm going home to the farm, to Lord Byron, to my job and... Stay on here until everything's settled with poor Reverend Charles. Take some time to think about your feelings, to decide what you really want."

"But I know what I want. I want a life with you and our child," Britt had said.

"Do you love me?"

"Why now, all of a sudden, is that so damned important? You gave me your virginity...you married me...you're having my child, and you never once had to hear the words."

"And I still don't have to hear the words." She had touched his face, that hard, rough face she so dearly loved. "But I want to know that the man I love, loves me. Maybe it's taken me a lifetime to finally realize that I deserve that much, that I'm worthy of being loved."

"Annie Rosie . . ."

He hadn't been able to say more. She'd driven the rental car back to Cherokee and left her husband in Riverton. If she were very lucky and God was very generous, the day might come when Britt could admit to himself that he loved her.

Twelve

Britt slammed the truck door, then turned and kicked it with his booted foot. The relentless rain drenched him to the skin. Issuing a few choice words, he stomped around to the back door and entered the kitchen, wiping his muddy feet on the throw rug that lay just inside the entrance. Wade sat at the table, a cup of coffee in one hand and the morning paper in the other.

Britt threw an envelope on the table, then hit it with his fist. Wade eyed his coffee cup, the contents still jostling from the vibration of the table against his elbow. "Bad news?" he asked, giving his brother a warm smile.

"It's the letter I sent to Anna Rose. She sent it back . . . unopened." Britt dropped down into the chair beside Wade, stretching out his long legs.

"She must want you to deliver any messages in person," Wade said.

"She's being totally irrational about this."

"Women who are nearly eight months pregnant have every right to act any way they want to," Wade said, folding the newspaper and laying it down beside his empty lunch plate. "Besides, I don't think she's asking for so much. All she wants is to be reassured that her husband loves her. Women are funny about stuff like that. Lydia even wants me to say the words when we're not making love. Can you imagine that?"

"Hell, Wade, this is no laughing matter. I will not go to her and say the words if I don't mean them, and how the hell do I know if I really love her or not?" Bracing his elbows on his knees, Britt slumped over and rested his chin on top of his clasped hands. "It seems like I loved Tanya all my life. Since we were kids."

"You had a boyish crush on Tanya that you let get out of hand just because you could never have her." Wade finished off the last drops of his coffee, then set the cup on the table. "You'd have gotten over that infatuation and fallen in love with somebody else if Paul hadn't been killed."

"What are you trying to say?"

"That you married Tanya out of guilt, not love. Because you were driving the car the night Paul was killed, you blamed yourself for his death, for Tanya's miscarriage and her attempted suicide. Maybe you still loved her, but I think, more than anything else, you pitied her."

The truth hurt, but then, maybe it should, Britt thought. Deep down inside, he'd known for a long time that what Wade had just said was the truth. But the feelings of pain and anger and bitterness with which he'd protected himself since Tanya's death were far more easily explainable if he'd loved his wife instead of simply pitied her.

"How the hell does a man know if he loves a woman?" Britt looked at his brother, hoping for an answer that would solve his problem.

Leaning over and chuckling, Wade slapped his brother on the shoulder. "You want me to go all soft and sloppy on you?"

"Yeah, if that's what it takes to explain."

"All right." Wade took in a deep breath, then ran his hand over his mouth and rubbed the stubble on his jaw. "She stays on your mind a lot. More than anything or anyone else. When you're away from her, you can't wait to be with her again. When she looks at you, you feel ten feet tall."

"Is that it?"

"You want her...hell, you get aroused just thinking about her. And no matter how good looking other women are or how attracted you might be to them, she's the only one you really want. No matter how many times you make love to her, you can never get enough of her."

"Yeah, I know exactly what you mean," Britt said.

"You want to take care of her and protect her and make her happy because she makes your life worth living."

"Damn!" Britt jumped up so quickly that he knocked over his chair.

"Who lit a fire under you?" Wade asked, grinning.

"I need to borrow some money, Wade. A couple of thousand maybe. I'll pay you back if it takes the rest of my life."

"What on earth are you going to do with two thousand bucks?"

"I'm going to buy my wife a ring, a sapphire ring as blue as her eyes."

"Anna Rose isn't the type to expect you to spend money on an expensive ring for her," Wade said.

"I know, but she's the type of woman who deserves it."

He'd had to take the back road to the farm. Days of pre-spring rain had flooded the only road coming in directly from Cherokee. The detour had cost him precious time. But he was here, finally. Home. He didn't recognize the vehicle in the drive, but assumed the shiny new red Blazer belonged to Anna Rose.

Checking his pocket for the sapphire and diamond ring he'd bought yesterday, he reached down on the seat, picked up the book of poetry that Lydia had helped him pick out and grabbed the huge bouquet of flowers he'd bought at the florist in Riverton.

With flowers in hand, Britt tucked the book under his coat before opening the door. Jumping out of his truck, he made a mad dash for the front porch. Slinging the moisture off his body, he tried the door. Locked. He rang the doorbell. No answer. He rang again. He delved into his pocket for the key, then inserted it in the lock and opened the front door.

"Anna Rose," he called out as he stepped inside the foyer. When he received no reply, he called out her name again.

Well, maybe she was in the kitchen and couldn't hear him for all the thunder. Damn, the electricity must be off again, he thought when he saw the kerosene lamp burning on the table at the end of the hall.

"Anna Rose, where are you?" He checked the living room, then walked through the dining room and into the kitchen. The rooms were empty. He'd started to turn around and head for the bedrooms when he heard Lord Byron's mournful howl. Where was the dog? His howl sounded as if it had come from the back porch.

After placing the bouquet and book of poetry on the kitchen table, Britt swung open the door leading to the porch. Lord Byron lay beside the open screen door, both his big paws resting atop the prone body lying half inside the porch and half outside on the steps. The rottweiler's soulful whine turned Britt's blood to ice.

"Anna Rose," he cried, rushing to her, going down on his knees to take her in his arms.

Her face was damp and stained with mud splatters. Her hair was soaking wet, as were her clothes. "Oh, Britt, I'm so glad to see you."

"What happened, honey? Are you hurt?"

"Help me . . . please, help me."

When he tried to lift her, she cried out in pain. "Tell me what happened. Did you fall?"

"The phone's dead . . . the electricity is out. I started having labor pains this morning." She clutched at her belly. "Maude's brother-in-law died yesterday. She left..." Anna Rose pulled her legs up to her stomach, crying out when another pain hit her. "She's in Chattanooga."

"I've got to get you up. Your legs and feet are lying out in the rain." Trying to ignore her moans, Britt lifted her in his arms. "The road's out into Cherokee, but I can take you to the Iuka hospital on the back roads, the way I came in."

Resting her head on his shoulder, she clung to him. "We'll never make it. I tried to get to the car, but . . . I was in such a hurry, I fell. The pains are every minute, now, and I can feel the baby's head trying to push out."

"Oh, God!" Carrying her inside, he made his way to their bedroom and lowered her to the bed. "Don't worry, Annie Rosie, I'm here and I'll take care of you."

"Have you ever delivered a baby?" she asked, then screamed when yet another labor pain struck.

The sound of her shrill scream and the look of anguish on her face sliced through Britt's heart, creating a shared pain within him. "No, but I've delivered calves and colts."

"Then you should have no problem delivering your own son, should you?"

"Let me help you get out of your clothes, honey. You're soaked to the skin." Without another minute's delay, he stripped her naked, then slipped on her robe, bunching it around her hips. "Better?" he asked.

"Warmer." She began breathing in hard, fast pants. "I'm afraid something might be wrong. I'm not due for another five weeks."

"I've heard first babies are always either late or early." Britt bent over the side of the bed and checked Anna Rose's condition. She was right—the baby's head was already in the birth canal.

Anna Rose felt tired, as if she'd been running a race, but she knew there would be no rest for her until the baby was born. Clutching the quilt on which Britt had laid her, she tried not to scream as pain sliced through her like a hot branding iron. Although the ache was low in her back, spreading to her abdomen, she could feel it all over. A body-racking pain that hurt more than anything she'd ever felt.

"Get some old sheets and a quilt out of the hall closet," she told him between contractions. "We...we can burn them after this is over. And...get some more towels out of the linen closet."

Britt hesitated leaving her. "You shouldn't be alone. What if—"

"Go on! Get the sheets and towels and quilt," she ordered. "And get a sharp knife out of the kitchen and sterilize it with the flame in one of the kerosene lamps."

Just as he left the room, he heard her scream again. Anna Rose wasn't the type of woman who endured pain meekly. He'd have to remember that if they ever decided to have another child. Oh, God, what was he thinking? *Please, Lord, just don't let anything happen to Anna Rose and this baby and I won't ask for another thing as long as I live.*

Carrying all the items she'd requested, Britt returned to the bedroom to find his wife drenched in sweat and repeating the word *tarnation* over and over again.

"Put that old quilt under me and then the towels. Save the clean sheets for the baby."

She felt an overwhelming need to push, a desperate urge to bear down. Her body arched upward as an enormous pressure built inside her, preparing her body for childbirth. She didn't know how much longer she could endure the pain, and she wondered how much longer Britt was going to be able to stand. He looked as if he were about to faint, and Anna Rose knew that the worst was yet to come.

Britt knelt between her spread thighs, watching, waiting as the baby's head emerged. "I can see the head. Push, honey. Push."

He didn't have to tell her to push! She wanted to tell him to just shut up and quit being so bossy. After all, she was perfectly capable of pushing without his orders.

Suddenly, nothing in the world existed except the life-giving force that controlled her body. Straining, Anna Rose cried out when, with a tremendous push, the pain began to ease as her body expelled its precious burden.

Britt guided the child out and into his arms, holding his son up so his mother could see him. Their son was round and fat and very dirty. Thick, black hair covered his little head.

"He's not crying," Anna Rose said. "What's wrong?"

"It's all right. He'll cry," Britt said, praying.

Laying the child atop Anna Rose's stomach, Britt quickly cut the cord, tied it off, then focused all his attention on his son—his son who wasn't breathing.

"Britt..."

Momentarily ignoring Anna Rose, Britt wiped off the baby's face and tried desperately to clean out his nose and mouth. *Breathe, son. Please breathe.*

"Oh, God, do something, Britt. He's dying." Using what little strength she had left, Anna Rose lifted her head to look down at where her husband was administering artificial respiration to their infant son.

The sound of a shrill, angry cry filled the bedroom. Britt, tears streaming down his face, held his child in his hands. "That's it, little man, cry for your mama. Let her know that you're all right."

When Britt handed their son to Anna Rose, he couldn't even see them, only the blurry outline of their faces and bodies. His vision was marred by tears.

Anna Rose opened her robe and held the squalling infant to her breast. He nuzzled her with his tiny nose. When she took his hand in hers, he curled his little fingers around her thumb.

So in awe of the new life she'd just delivered into the world, Anna Rose didn't even look at Britt until she heard his muffled moans. Turning her head toward the sound, she cried out, so touched by the sight of Britt on his knees beside her bed. He laid his head against her hip. Racked with tears, his big body trembled from the force of his unchecked emotions.

"Britt, it's all right. We're both fine." She placed her hand on his head, running her fingers lovingly through his hair.

Raising his head, he stared at her, then lifted himself enough to reach out and touch her face. "I love you, Anna Rose. More than anything on this earth."

There was something so powerful about a strong man's tears, Anna Rose thought as she smiled at her husband. "It took you long enough to come to your senses, Britt Cameron."

David Palmer Cameron and his mother came home from the hospital three days later amid the chaos of a family celebration that extended to include Anna Rose's long-time friends and neighbors.

With Grandma Ruthie installed in the guest bedroom for an extended visit, Britt turned over the care of his son to her until David's next feeding. There had never been any question in Anna Rose's mind that she would breast-feed, but she promised Britt that, as soon as David was old enough for fruit juice, he would be allowed to give him his bottle.

"I don't feel the least bit tired, Britt," Anna Rose said when her husband laid her down on their bed. "I just had a baby, you know, I'm not an invalid."

"Humor me." He sat down beside her. "It's not every day a woman gives me a child. So quit trying to boss everybody around and let me run this show."

"You brought me in here for a reason, didn't you?"

"For privacy," he admitted.

"Well, as much as I'd like to indulge in a little lustful lovemaking, I'm afraid there are parts of my body not quite ready for—"

He laughed. God, what a woman. His woman. "Annie Rosie . . . Annie Rosie." He couldn't stop laughing.

"What's so funny?" She sat up in the bed.

He pushed her back down, hovering over her. "You are."

"I am not."

He pulled a tiny jeweler's box out of his pocket, flipped it open and stuck it in Anna Rose's face.

"What's this?" she asked, trying again to sit up.

"It's your engagement ring."

"But we're married."

"I bought it before I left Riverton." He lifted the jeweled circle from its velvet cushion and held it out to her. "I love you, Anna Rose. Will you marry me? Will you come live with me and be my love . . . forever?"

Wiping away tears of joy, Anna Rose held out her left hand for him to slip the ring onto her finger. "Yes."

Britt nudged her over. Lying down beside her, he took her in his arms. And that's the way Grandma Ruthie found them an hour later when she brought a hungry David Cameron to his mother.

Epilogue

The Palmer-Cameron farm had played host to an annual Fourth of July picnic for the past five years, and this year was no exception. Friends and family filled the yard. Children of all ages and sizes ran helter-skelter everywhere. Roy Dean and his amateur band filled the hot summer air with the sounds of bluegrass, rich with fiddle music.

Just as she stepped out the back door, a pie in each hand, Anna Rose felt Britt's arm go around her as he took one of the pies. He patted the side of her stomach. "I'll bet no one suspects you're pregnant. Let's make an announcement?"

"Do you really think anyone will be interested in the fact that there's a third little Cameron on the way?"

"The folks in Cherokee, Alabama, are always interested in the latest news. Besides, the birth of my first daughter is going to be a media event."

A dozen picnic tables had been set up beneath a grove of century-old oak trees. Ruthie Cameron sat wiping ice cream off three-year-old Daniel Cameron's mouth, much to his aggravation, while five-year-old David fed his hot dog to Lord Byron.

Wade and Lydia had taken their children down to the pond where a small crowd was swimming. Cousins Opal and Maude were taking turns giving Kyle Ross instructions on the proper way to crank an ice cream maker, while his pregnant wife Tracy watched with barely concealed amusement.

"There's not a soul in the house right now," Britt said. "Who would know if we slipped away for a little while?"

"Britt Cameron, are you suggesting that you want to make love to me in the middle of the day with at least sixty people visiting?"

"Yeah."

"Don't be silly."

He gave her a little-boy pouty look. "Tired of me already?"

"Quite the contrary." She set the pie down on the table filled with desserts. He did the same. Turning, she threw her arms around his neck, then ran her fingers across his smooth cheek. After his plastic surgery four years ago, he had shaved his beard but left the mustache. "I have definite plans for tonight . . . down at the pond . . . a private party."

"Tell me more," he said.

"Well, first we'll take off all our clothes and go skinny-dipping. We'll kiss awhile and play around a bit, and then . . ."

"And then?"

"And then I'm going to . . ." She told him in simple, explicit terms exactly what she was going to do to him.

"Annie Rosie . . . Annie Rosie . . . wherever did you learn such language?"

* * * * *

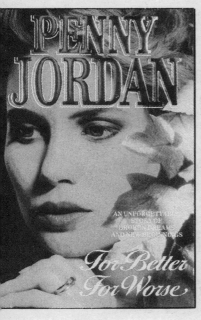

COMING NEXT MONTH

THE SEDUCER
Linda Turner

Jake Knight had been framed and he needed the help of an investigator with the highest social connections, he needed the help of old flame Zoe Murdock. But he hated to ask her...

WHITEHORN'S WOMAN
Barbara McCauley

Jonas Whitehorn had loved and lost. Now all he had was his grandfather and he wasn't going to let Brook Devlin manipulate the old man. Jonas, on the other hand, would quite like to manipulate Brook!

SWEET GEORGIA GAL
Emilie Richards

Ryan Cunningham needed help when he became the guardian of his four nieces and nephews, and beauty queen Stacey McDonald was perfect for the job. She would be a wonderful wife and mother...

Silhouette Desire

COMING NEXT MONTH

NIGHT OF LOVE
Diana Palmer

Man of the Month Steven Ryker was prepared to go to any lengths to reclaim former fiancée Meg Shannon. But could Steven's plan for one night of love evolve into a lifetime of happiness?

BALANCED
Lass Small

Tim Bolt thought playing chaperon to Carol Brown would be easy. But he seemed to be single-handedly protecting this woman from every lustful male in Chicago, and she didn't even appreciate it!

KANE'S WAY
Dixie Browning

Kane Smith took one look at Aurora Hubbard and knew that he couldn't let her marry the wrong man; she'd be miserable. In fact, unless she married Kane, *he* was going to be miserable!

COMING NEXT MONTH FROM

Silhouette

Sensation

*romance with a special mix of
suspense, glamour and drama*

WORTH ANY RISK Kathleen Korbel
SNOWFIRE Heather Graham Pozzessere
TOO GOOD TO FORGET Marilyn Tracy
LIAR'S MOON Anne Wilson

Special Edition

*longer, satisfying romances with
mature heroines and lots of emotion*

MORE THAN HE BARGAINED FOR Carole Halston
COMMANDO Lindsay McKenna
GROOM WANTED Debbie Macomber
FAMILY MATTERS Marie Ferrarella
BORN INNOCENT Christine Rimmer
HOLD BACK THE NIGHT Linda Barlow

Four Silhouette Desires absolutely free!

Provocative and sensual love stories for the sophisticated reader. A highly charged blend of forceful characters and daring storylines set the scene for exciting encounters and unpredictable reactions.

Now you can enjoy four Silhouette Desires as your free gift from Reader Service, plus the opportunity to enjoy six brand new titles delivered direct to your door every single month!

Turn the page for details of how to apply and claim more free gifts!

An irresistible offer from Silhouette

Here's your personal invitation from Silhouette to become a regular reader of Desires. And to welcome you, we'd like you to have four books, a cuddly teddy and a special mystery gift - absolutely FREE and without obligation!

Then, every month look forward to receiving six Silhouette Desires delivered to your door for just £1.70 each. Postage and packing is FREE! Plus our FREE Newsletter featuring authors, competitions, special offers and lots more...

This invitation comes with no strings attached. You may cancel or suspend your subscription at any time and still keep your FREE books and gifts.

It's so easy. Send no money now but simply complete the coupon below and return it today to :-

Silhouette Reader Service, FREEPOST, PO Box 236, Croydon, Surrey CR9 9EL

NO STAMP REQUIRED ✂

Please rush me 4 FREE Silhouette Desires and 2 FREE gifts! Please also reserve me a Reader Service subscription. If I decide to subscribe, I can look forward to receiving 6 brand new Desires for only £10.20 each month. Postage and packing is FREE and so is my monthly Newsletter. If I choose not to subscribe, I shall write to you within 10 days and still keep my FREE books and gifts. I may cancel or suspend my subscription at any time simply by writing to you. I am over 18 years of age. Please write in BLOCK CAPITALS

Ms/Mrs/Miss/Mr _____ EP67S

Address _____

_____

_____ Postcode _____

Signature _____